24

BLUE FALLS

A JAKE PETTMAN THRILLER BY

WES MARKIN

CONTENTS

ABOUT THE AUTHOR

Wes Markin is the bestselling author of the DCI Yorke crime novels set in Salisbury. His latest series, The Yorkshire Murders, stars the compassionate and relentless DCI Emma Gardner. He is also the author of the Jake Pettman thrillers set in New England. Wes lives in Harrogate with his wife and two children, close to the crime scenes in The Yorkshire Murders.

You can find out more at:

www.wesmarkinauthor.com

facebook.com/wesmarkinauthor

BY WES MARKIN

DCI Yorke Thrillers

One Last Prayer

The Repenting Serpent

The Silence of Severance

Rise of the Rays

Dance with the Reaper

Christmas with the Conduit

Better the Devil

A Lesson in Crime

Jake Pettman Thrillers

The Killing Pit

Fire in Bone

Blue Falls

The Rotten Core

Rock and a Hard Place

The Yorkshire Murders

The Viaduct Killings

The Lonely Lake Killings

The Cave Killings

Details of how to claim your **FREE** DCI Michael Yorke quick read, **A lesson in Crime**, can be found at the end of this book.

Text copyright © 2021 Wes Markin

First published 2021

ISBN: 9798467751481

Imprint: Dark Heart Publishing

Edited by Brian Paone

Cover design by Cherie Foxley

For Jenny and David

ON THE DAY JAKE PETTMAN LEAVES BLUE FALLS

13:18

BLOOD RAN INTO Jake Pettman's eyes. He leaned on his rented Ford's hood—it was that or go arse over tit—and surveyed the bent fender.

A deep voice behind him asked, "You okay?"

He held up his hand to signal he was, then felt the hand on his shoulder; the Samaritan had not bought his bullshit. Feeling some steadiness return, Jake abandoned his smoking hood and stood upright, forcing the man's hand to fall away. "I need your help."

Jake's Samaritan was seventy-plus, but his tense and eager pose suggested he would be as effective as a man half his age. *Good. Time is running out.*

Jake used his sleeve to rub blood from his eyes. "What's the time, *exactly*?"

"Eighteen minutes past one."

Fuck. Jake slammed a fist on his crumpled hood. *Fuck ... fuck ...* "I'm out of time." He eyed his vehicle. *Bastard car.* The crash must have put him under for almost ten minutes. He regarded the elderly man again and shielded his eyes. The summer sun was coming in strong. Jake spied the old red Buick the man had arrived in. The door was open, and the engine was still running. "I need you to take me to the top of Ross Hill."

1

"If I take you anywhere, son, I'm taking you to the hospital."

"That's not an option."

"It's the only option. You're at death's door—"

Jake stepped forward.

The old man recoiled but struck a pugnacious pose. "You're not thinking clearly, son."

You got that right. Which is why I'm not brushing you aside. Jake looked at the Buick again. *I don't think I could aim that beast straight right now.* Jake scanned an empty highway framed by cornfields. "I'm not the bad guy here. You need to take me up there." He pointed to the summit of Ross Hill. "Before anybody dies." He nodded at the Buick. "I don't think me and your old girl are going to get on all that well, but I'll give it a whirl if I have to."

The old man sighed. "Well then, I'm driving. She's the only family I got."

Fighting back a wave of nausea, Jake said, "We need to leave right now."

The old man nodded. "Get in, then, but you better be the good guy."

Jake only stumbled once as he approached the Buick. He was optimistic that control was finding its way back to him. Jesus, he hoped so. God only knows what awaited him at the top of Ross Hill. Jake opted for the back seat, believing he would remain more threatening than riding shotgun.

The elderly man passed an oil-stained rag to him. "Sorry, it's all I have." He patted the wheel. "But it serves my baby well when she's bleeding."

"It'll serve me well too, thanks." Jake pressed it to his leaking forehead. "But we have to hurry."

The old man responded and exited the highway onto

the dirt path up Ross Hill. "What are we going to find up there?"

Jake felt his nausea build but took it as a good sign that his adrenaline was ramping up. "You mean, what will *I* find, old man. You'll be staying well back."

"It sounds like you're going to war."

"If I'm too late, you can bet I will be."

His cellphone beeped. He cast the rag aside, slipped the cell from his pocket, and read the message: *I warned you.* The cell beeped again. Jake opened the photograph with a trembling finger. The phone slipped from his hand. He took a deep breath, desperately trying to process what he had just seen. He clenched his hands, focused on the roof of the car, then roared. At the same time, he punched the back of the passenger seat again ... and again.

"War it is then," the old man said.

12:59

JAKE'S SPEEDOMETER RACED past ninety as he cleared the crossroads.

The driver of one vehicle screeched to a halt, while the driver of another possessed the sound reflexes to screech around Jake's Ford.

Jake had no time to reflect on how lucky he was to survive—neither did a moment exist for him to ponder the chances of him facing one of his worst fears again less than a week after the last time. High-speed driving wasn't for everyone. It certainly wasn't for Jake Pettman.

There was no time because, in this moment, existed an even greater fear for Jake. The death of someone *close* to him. The death of someone *because* of him.

With his horn, he warned several vehicles that he was about to attempt the unthinkable, swung to the other side of the road, and cleared them.

Their expressions as he passed were a mix of disgust and disbelief.

He was thankful that no vehicle intercepted him on the wrong side of the road—not because of his own survival but because the survival of another depended on his imminent arrival at Ross Hill.

As he cleared the rotary in which he'd almost killed an unseated biker days before, Jake checked his cellphone mounted on the windshield. ETA was 13:12, but that was calculated at the speed limit he was currently ignoring, so hopefully, he'd buy himself more time.

He looked at the clock on the dash—13:02. He had sixteen minutes until ... until ...

Someone close to him died because of what he once was.

He pushed his speedometer to a hundred as he approached the bridge that cut over the Skweda into Sharon's Edge.

Déjà vu.

Five days earlier, he'd hit this bridge at a similar speed. He'd drawn so close to the bumper of Chief Gabriel Jewell's Audi that he could taste his exhaust fumes. Gabriel was a cold-blooded killer who needed shutting down, but ...

Kayla MacLeoid, a fourteen-year-old girl, had been locked in his trunk.

Jake had abandoned the chase after the phone call which informed him of this. But not this time. This was one journey Jake wouldn't abandon. *Couldn't abandon.* He turned off the bridge and negotiated several roads at breakneck speed. Eventually, he turned onto a highway that speared into a rural area of cornfields.

In this direction, the sunlight intensified. He slammed down the sun visor. It didn't help. He squinted and kept his foot down. Another glance at his cell now showed his ETA to be 13:11. He'd bought himself an extra minute.

He checked the clock again—13:08.

Close. In fact, he could see the hill looming ahead on the right. The turnoff was close. He knew what he was looking for. A yard-high rock wearing the painted words: *The Summit of Ross Hill.* It was time to start slowing for the sudden turn—

A loud boom made him flinch. The car jerked to the right. The taste of bile made him wince. His death was close ... *her* death was close. He'd never experienced a blowout, and every single nerve ending burned as he lived his worst nightmare, but he desperately held onto the words of advice his best friend, Michael Yorke, had once given him. *"Grip that steering wheel like your life depends on it, because it does. And avoid the brakes. Hit them and you'll spin. Let the car slow gradually."*

The pull on the car was like nothing Jake had ever experienced. He stared out the window over his glowing white knuckles as the car was sucked back and forth from a straight path. He let the car slow naturally, but it wasn't happening fast enough. Then the car felt as if it was being yanked. He saw the yard-high stone that pointed to the summit of Ross Hill racing to meet him head on.

12:53

UNABLE TO FULLY comprehend what he'd just seen, Jake stumbled from the house and steadied himself against the porch railing.

He caught a glimpse of a large brown-gray squirrel scurrying up one of the trees on the road opposite the house. He followed its path until only its orangey-brown underside was visible from way up high, then it was gone. It was a creature extremely accomplished at disappearing, at evading its predators.

Jake, on the other hand, was anything but. There was no escape for prey like him. Three thousand miles from home. A town in the middle of nowhere. And still, he'd been found.

He threw up over the side of the railing. Wiping his mouth with his sleeve, he turned to look at the open door of the house. Then, he fully acknowledged what he'd just seen inside that room.

Death.

And the inescapable conclusion that no matter where he, Jake Pettman, went, death would surely follow, and everything he loved would be lost.

His cellphone beeped. The message came from a number not stored in his directory: *I hunt from way up high.*

With hands still trembling from the discovery in the living room, he tried desperately to reply to quiz the sender about his identity, but he didn't get far before the next message came through: *The world looks up to me. You look up to me.*

Jake shook the cellphone. "Fuck off! Who're you? What do you want from me?"

Beep. *Ross Hill. Through the Broken Rocks and to the edge. Come, Jake, and look up to me.*

Jake felt the corners of his mouth twitching as he thought, *Is this the person? The person responsible for that abomination in this house?* The likelihood of this being the killer sent a burst of adrenaline through Jake, which steadied his shaking hand. He managed to rattle off his reply, *Why don't you come and hunt here, prick? We can discuss what you've done.*

He paced the porch, waiting for the reply.

Beep. *I hunt where I please. This world is mine. I do not argue for what is my right. Twenty-five minutes, Jake. Not a second more.*

Jake clenched his teeth as he punched in his reply. *Fuck you. My terms. I'm standing where you left your last mess.* He stared at the screen, waiting for the murderous bastard to consent. No reply came, so Jake took that as a sign that the prick had accepted his counter invitation. He leaned against the railing again and tried to sight the evasive squirrel. He didn't but spoke out loud to the animal anyway. "The difference between us is I'm done running."

His cellphone beeped. He opened a photograph. He pulled so hard on the railing with his single hand that he heard it splinter. The photograph showed Piper Goodwin slumped in her wheelchair. Her head hung forward, and her dark hair streamed over her face and into her lap.

Jake took his hand from the railing before he broke it.

She was perched at a cliff edge.

His cellphone beeped. *My little eyas. It is almost time to take her from her nest so she can fly too. Twenty-four minutes now, Jake. Not a second more.*

1

FIVE DAYS BEFORE JAKE PETTMAN LEAVES BLUE FALLS

SKULKING IN THE shadow of a cluster of red spruces, Chief of Police Gabriel Jewell popped another instant-release Adderall, followed by another piece of gum.

Gabriel shook the bottle he'd stolen long ago from Niles Waters, a man who suffered from both ADHD and alcoholism and had spent the night in the Blue Falls drunk tank during one of Gabriel's shifts.

The bottle sounded light. He'd have to slow down his intake, taper off, or he'd be hitting an almighty brick wall within days. He'd need to sustain his energy levels until he'd fled Rosstown plantation good and proper.

His life, and—he listened to the thumping from the trunk—the life of Kayla Macleoid depended on it. The noise of Kayla pounding the trunk was starting to irritate him. It seemed to be finding rhythm with a pounding in his temples.

He took several deep breaths and leaned against the car, waiting for both the sun to set and the headache to ease. When it was clear the headache was going nowhere, he turned his attention to his next move.

He reached into the back seat for his rifle, which he'd collected during that flying visit home after executing Priscilla Stone. Then he went around to the trunk. He tapped the trunk with the butt of the rifle and the thumping stopped. "I'm opening the trunk. Don't be acting like a cornered animal."

She didn't respond.

He took no chances and was careful to pop the trunk with his rifle readied.

The fourteen-year-old girl was lying on her side. Her hair was unkempt, and he could tell from the smell that she'd wet herself on the journey. "If you were going to kill me, I'd be dead already."

"That was true ... before. The equation has changed somewhat." He chewed hard on the gum. He wanted so desperately to reach out and stroke her face. It was red from crying. It pained him to see her this way. "I'd prefer to do this with you though. It'd be safer and easier alone, but that's not what I want. Never has been. I've never wanted to be alone since ..."

"Your sister died?" Kayla snarled.

Gabriel nodded. "Yes, but especially since that night you came to me for help."

"Yes, for help! Not to be locked in your basement. Not to be locked in the trunk of your car. For help, you evil bastard. *For help*."

"Which I gave you."

"By killing my family?"

"There was no other way. There never is with people like that. I took care of you. I gave you books. I never touched you ... not like that."

"But you wanted to." She narrowed her eyes. "*Still* want to."

Gabriel flinched.

"And that won't change, will it?"

"You have my word that it will. I know the truth of my sister now. Those who caused her death are gone. I am going to start afresh ... with you. I *will* change."

Kayla snorted. "I've seen you. You'll never be able to control yourself. You are like one of my father's dogs in heat."

"Shut up."

Kayla tried to sit upright.

Gabriel pressed the muzzle against her chest. "Don't. Not until I've explained what's happening. You need to listen, and you need to listen carefully."

Kayla slumped back. "If you let me out of this trunk, I'll do whatever you say, I promise."

"That's a start, Kayla, and I believe you. Because no matter what you think of me, whatever you *believe* I am capable of, you need to know that if you let me, I'll protect you. And all those around you, all those you think you can trust, they are liars—you know what your father was, the *things* he did. You really think that those back in Blue Falls will protect you? Forgive you for what your father did to them? You think they can ever love you like I love you?"

She shook her head. "No."

Gabriel smiled and, just for a moment, chose to believe she was sincere, that she wasn't just telling him what he wanted to hear, and it felt truly wonderful. So, before the tendrils of doubt could begin to weave around his thoughts again, he moved swiftly on to the plan of action. "We leave the car here. We cannot escape Rosstown by road. They will have the interstate blocked, so we lay low until I can make arrangements."

"Where will we go?"

"Sit up now, Kayla, and I'll show you." Gabriel took several steps backward as Kayla obeyed. "Please. Climb out of the car." Once she was standing before him, he lowered the rifle to his side. "Don't make me regret this, Kayla."

"I won't."

Again, he enjoyed her sincerity, despite the pounding in his temples that had continued to beat irrespective of Kayla's thumping. He wondered if his headache was acting as a warning about offering this girl any kind of trust—or maybe it was just time to slow down on the uppers.

He pointed to a house in the distance. "We've come a good way to the outskirts of Sharon's Edge. I know the woman who lives in that house on that small farm. Her name is Molly, and she's nice. But she cannot know the truth, Kayla, not until she hears it on the news. Until that point, you must let me do all the talking, and then, when I have the chance, I can incapacitate her. No one else needs to get hurt. You are a large part of making that so. Do you understand?"

Kayla stared at the house in the distance and thought for a moment, then faced Gabriel and nodded.

"Thank you. Let's go."

As Gabriel and Kayla approached the Cape Cod-styled farmhouse, a couple of dogs in the distance expressed their discontent.

"Nothing to worry about," Gabriel said, nodding at the rifle's strap across his chest.

"I'm not worried about the dogs."

Gabriel nodded. Fair point. Why would she be? She had been raised on a farm full of fighting dogs.

While crossing the field, Gabriel stayed close to her. He hadn't bought her bullshit guarantee to behave back at the car. He sighted her eyes darting back and forth as she undoubtably considered her best route to freedom.

"I want to say sorry for hurting you," Gabriel said, "the other night when you tried to run." He'd bashed her head off his driveway and knocked her clean out. He'd mentioned it to remind her of the consequences of fleeing but did actually feel apologetic as he spoke the words. He hated hurting her.

"You had no choice."

Contrition. More bullshit. "Thanks for being so understanding, Kayla. And when I lost control earlier, when I came to you, wanting to, *you know,* I'm sorry; that wasn't me."

She moved her head so he couldn't see her eyes.

"Things were taking their toll. My sister, Mason Rogers, all of that ... but I feel clearer now that I know what we have to do. Listen, Kayla, I know you don't believe me, but regardless of what you said back at the car about me being a dog in heat, I won't ever touch you like that again. Are you listening?"

He waited a moment and was about to show his discontent with a sigh when she nodded. "Yes."

Despite knowing deep down that she would never trust

him and would probably kill him if she had the chance, he accepted this for the time being.

Gravel crunched underfoot when they hit a long driveway. Together, they closed in on the white-washed, single-story building, and Gabriel was relieved that none of the noisy dogs met them on route. The large pen alongside the house had kept them from harm's way.

They climbed the steps onto the covered white porch. He looked down at Kayla, who remained close to his right side. "Wait here."

She nodded, sidestepped, and leaned against the railing.

"And remember, her life is in your hands."

The front door opened before Gabriel had the chance to ring the doorbell.

Molly had always been in good shape but not like this. A light-blue sleeveless blouse revealed impressive sinewy arms. He watched her lean muscles twitch as she tensed her grip on a shotgun.

"Have you forgotten I'm the chief of police, Molly?" Gabriel nodded at the shotgun while praying he had not yet made the news—and if he had, that she'd not seen it.

"No. Have you forgotten you're not fucking welcome?" She glanced Kayla standing by the railing. "What's happening?"

"She's with me."

"Why?"

"Let us both in, and I'll explain."

She shook her head. "Impossible." She looked at Kayla again. "Another prisoner to your secrets and lies?"

"I don't know what you're talking—"

"She can come in. You can't."

So distracted by the impressive muscles on her defined body, Gabriel hadn't noticed, until this moment, that her

13

eyelids and lips were spasming. He took a deep breath. Was Molly capable of pulling that trigger? She hadn't been way back when, but now? She certainly *seemed* very different. And that made her very unpredictable.

"That's not an option, Molly."

"The only option, Gabriel. We're done. Have been for a long time. You told me you were a man of your word, remember?"

"Yes, I remember, but things have changed. I'm in a situation now that I can't handle alone—"

"You should have thought about—"

"*Listen*, Molly. I'm perfectly aware that your family no longer owes me. And after your help, things will return to normal, but a desperate man will resort to desperate measures. Help me, and the secret about who you are remains just that. A secret."

She narrowed her eyes and lifted the shotgun.

"Gunning me down on your doorstep is not the best way for you to keep flying below the radar."

She lowered the shotgun. "Lucky for you, then, that you left me with a speck of willpower all those years back." Molly marched onto her porch.

Gabriel stepped backward to allow her past.

She slipped her arm around Kayla. "What's your name?"

"Kayla."

Molly froze and eyed Gabriel. "Kayla *MacLeoid*?"

"Yes," Kayla said.

"Jesus, Gabriel. The missing girl?"

"She's alive, isn't she? Not like the rest of her family. Try not to judge before you know the full story."

Molly shook her head. "You brought *this* to my doorstep?"

"Ironic comment considering the things I *cleaned* off your doorstep in the past."

"I paid for it all."

"You did, yes. Feed us, let me explain what is going on, and we'll be gone before we get any dirt on your sacred doorstep."

Molly led Kayla into the house. "Come on, dear. I've just made soup."

―――――

At the kitchen table, Kayla attacked her bowl of clam chowder like a wild animal.

Gabriel stared at his bowl but was yet to take a mouthful.

"Not eating?" Molly asked, leaning by the kitchen sink while watching her guests eat.

"No appetite."

"Ahh ... What are you taking, Gabriel?"

He furrowed his brows at her. "Why do you ask that?"

"The fact that you haven't stopped chewing since you came to my door."

"I *like* gum."

"You're also pale and speaking at a hundred miles an hour."

"Having a shotgun waved at you will do that to a man."

"You're wired, Gabriel. Admit it."

Gabriel spat his gum onto the table and took several mouthfuls of chowder. "Happy?"

Molly shrugged. "Tell me what you've got me mixed up in."

Gabriel gave her the only information she needed. Kayla had come to him for help following her father's murderous exploits and that he'd been her protector since. He stared at Kayla as he spoke, reminding her of his earlier message.

Her life is in your hands.

"So why can't she move on with her life now? Her father's gone."

"But not the brother. Not Ayden," Gabriel lied. He'd ended that young man's life in his basement. "He's hunting her, and she needs to be as far from wandering eyes as possible. Your place fitted the bill."

Molly grunted. "So, now what?"

He took another spoonful of chowder. Despite his loss of appetite, he could appreciate the taste. "This is good—"

"*Now* what?"

"We lie low for a few days. Then I will find Ayden and lock him down while you take care of Kayla."

Molly wandered toward Kayla with the pan and spooned more chowder into her empty bowl. "Is this true, dear?"

Gabriel stared, wide-eyed, at Kayla.

She caught his look and nodded at Molly. "Yes, ma'am."

Molly stared back at Gabriel. "Sounds like bullshit to me."

Gabriel shrugged and took another mouthful.

Molly turned her back to her two guests and started to clean the dishes.

He gave Kayla a grateful nod. At first, she appeared like she would burst into tears, which caused Gabriel's heart to quicken, but she returned to gorging on the chowder, and Gabriel felt some relief.

Gabriel sat back in his chair for a while. He'd had about half the chowder but wouldn't force any more food down his throat. He'd already made his gesture of good will. He watched Kayla work her way through another bowl, nodding with satisfaction as she built her strength.

Then he turned his eyes on Molly, who was pottering around her kitchen, tidying. Starting at the fiery-red hair, he ran his gaze over the woman he'd spent so much time with in her younger years. Her muscular physique was interesting. He let his focus linger on her strong, defined calves and wondered if he could still feel aroused in her company, like he had done when she was fourteen. He decided he might try later when he'd incapacitated her. To form a sexual connection with a woman in her twenties would be healthy and a sure sign he was healing. It would give him confidence that he could wait until Kayla was older before he suggested they take their relationship to the next level.

When they'd been at the table for over thirty minutes and everyone seemed calm, it was a perfect opportunity to make his move. After Molly had taken Kayla's bowl to the sink to wash it, he placed a finger to his lips at Kayla. He rose to his feet, and a strange sensation began.

The world tilted back and forth.

He steadied himself against the table and shook his head. It seemed to help, but then he detected a weakness beginning in his legs.

Molly turned from the kitchen sink, holding a knife in front of her.

"You bitch!"

"I was worried it wouldn't work. You haven't eaten much—"

With one hand, he propelled himself sideways into her. It was a risk with that blade there, but so was waiting for whatever she'd drugged him with to take a firmer hold. His bodyweight smashed the air from her, and he felt her hot breath spear his cheek. He glanced down, half-expecting to see the knife sticking from his numbing body, but was relieved to see that wasn't the case and that her arm was now pinned against the work surface.

When he lifted his eyes to her face, he experienced that peculiar tilting of his surroundings again and felt his legs tremble. He wouldn't have control of himself for too much longer. He stepped backward while thrusting his left elbow into her right cheek.

Her head snapped up and left, allowing Gabriel the time to slam his fist into her stomach.

He bellowed when his knuckles cracked against the work surface. The wily bitch had either evaded him or he was fast losing all coordination. He prepared to strike again with his damaged hand, except a burning sensation took hold, and he stumbled backward.

The knife was sticking out of his upper left arm.

He reached for the knife handle as he stumbled. "Clever girl ..."

She came in a blur, and he felt her knee in his guts. He gagged, and while he desperately sought out air, she came again. This time, her foot crunched into one of his shins, and rather than risk a broken leg, he moved with the blow and lost his footing. He saw the kitchen table rushing toward him. Facedown on the ground, he heard the upended table crash down nearby. Everything was spinning now, but he could see Kayla's sneakers.

"Run, Kayla!" Molly shouted.

Gabriel grabbed Kayla's ankle with his left hand as she attempted to flee, bringing her to the ground too. He heard her cry out, but he doubted she was in as much pain as him; he'd just restrained her with the arm that had been knifed.

He heard a thud and felt a burning pain in the center of his back.

"Get off her!"

He felt Molly's foot smash into the center of his back again and again. The pain was useful; it kept excessive grogginess at bay. Keeping hold of the flailing girl's ankle with one hand, he reached with his other to the handle of the knife in his upper left arm. He yelled as he slipped it free.

He released Kayla and rolled onto his back. His stupid hostess continued ploughing him with kicks, so he grabbed the offending limb and dragged her on top of him.

They drew close for the first time in many years, except, despite being just as *electric*, this contact was for entirely different reasons. He heard the clicking of her teeth as she weaponized them, but before she could lock them to his nose, he slammed a fist into the side of her head and pushed her from him. He then rolled again so he was on her back.

Lying over her with his cheek pressed against hers, he heard her plead. "Please ... please."

He raised himself onto one arm and lifted the kitchen knife as high as he could manage.

"Please—"

He slammed down the knife. It didn't feel as if he had much strength left, so he was surprised the blade slid so easily through the back of her skull.

Molly convulsed several times before going still.

He heard the front door slam and turned to look at the open kitchen door.

Kayla had fled.

After managing to get to his feet, drunk on whatever Molly had tried to knock him out with, he grabbed his rifle from beside the chair he'd been sitting in before all hell had broken loose. With his legs feeling like jelly, he staggered from the kitchen into the hallway. He reached the front door, despite having to steady himself against the wall a few times, and saw Kayla running in the distance. He sighed. He could never catch her in this state.

He slipped to his knees and raised his rifle. "This is on you, Molly, you stupid bitch." He aimed at the girl he'd adored since the moment she'd knocked on his door, begging for his help. His arms were weak and shaky under the influence of the chowder's secret ingredient.

He fired.

Birds rose from the trees.

Kayla continued to run.

Fuck. He'd never hit her in this state. Blood ran over his hands, and he glanced at his red-drenched sleeve. He took a deep breath, lifted the gun, and sighted Kayla again. *Steady ... Steady ...* No fucking chance.

He fired.

No birds this time, but Kayla *did* fall.

2

THE DAY BEFORE JAKE PETTMAN LEAVES BLUE FALLS

PIPER GOODWIN PLACED her crutches against the wall and lay on the bed. She groaned as she adjusted herself into a comfortable position.

Jake sat on the edge of the bed beside her.

She stroked his leg. "A kiss goodnight?"

"It's not nighttime!"

"Okay, Mr. Pedantic, a kiss before my powernap?"

"More like it." Jake leaned in for a kiss and felt her tongue press against his.

After he broke it off, she lifted her eyebrows. "Rejection? Haven't had to deal with that since high school."

"Wow, really? That's some run. You must be quite the catch."

"Clearly not for you."

Jake smiled and sat on the side of the bed. "Definitely for me, but there are two problems. *That*." He pointed at her bandaged leg. "Think of the stitches. And also *this*." He used the palms of his hands to gesture around the room.

"By *this*, do you mean my childhood bedroom?"

"Precisely that."

Piper laughed. "But I'm no longer a child."

"Your mother is downstairs."

"And we're upstairs ..." She reached over and stroked his thigh.

Jake took her hand in his, lifted it from the area into which it was creeping, and held it between the palms of his hands. "Still ... she is rather god-fearing."

"She's not going to walk in!"

"Let's not chance it. Besides, I like staying on your couch in the study. Being kicked out and returning to a motel would be a disaster. Anyway, changing the subject, you've still not told me what the trip was like."

"Trip? You make it sound like a vacation. I visited my mentally ill biological mother."

"Sorry, I didn't mean—"

"Don't worry! It was much better than last time. Amber is still dazed, confused. The doctor said this will most likely always be the case. I guess it's for the best though, right? Why would we want her to recall that pit or the postpartum psychosis which made her, you know, do what she did?"

Jake squeezed her hand and nodded.

"There are many quiet moments, but sometimes she comes alive, rather like an excitable child, and she talks about her schooldays, which are a far cry from the hell she ended up marrying into."

The hell she married into, of course, had been that heinous world of Piper's biological father, Jotham

MacLeoid. Unbeknownst to Piper, this had been the man Jake had executed to free Blue Falls from his vile grip.

Piper wiped a tear from her eye. "Sorry."

"Don't apologise. *Never* apologise."

"Okay. She's all I have now. I doubt anyone, other than the doctors, will give her the time of day. I don't think she ever truly knew what she was doing." She sighed. "Do you think people will ever truly accept mental illness?"

"Some will, some won't, I guess. They seemed more accepting back where I come from."

"Everywhere is more accepting than Blue Falls."

Jake nodded. Wasn't that the truth. Just look what had happened to Mason Rogers' gravestone yesterday. He'd led a tormented life, flicking between personalities. Yes, one of those personalities had been downright malicious and had led to the damage on Piper's leg, but this man was gone now. He was a tortured soul at peace, so why desecrate his resting place and attempt to exhume the remains? The police had been forced to move a dead body to a secret location; that's how accepting Blue Falls was of mental illness.

"Some people will be horrified at how happy Amber seems."

"They would. Yes."

"But it's as if those things—those horrendous things she did—were done by someone else. Not her."

Jake nodded. "Yet, that would rile some even more, the fact she's not taking responsibility for what she did."

"How can she take responsibility for something she cannot *remember?*"

Jake stroked her face. "You don't have to tell me. I hear you."

She took his hand and pulled him closer toward her.

Another kiss. Another flick of the tongue. "I need you.. Now ..."

"For distraction?" Jake pulled back with a raised eyebrow.

"Yes, but is it so bad to be distracted by someone you love?"

Jake leaned forward for a kiss.

Afterward, there were no tangled sheets, damp bodies, or gulps of air. Their lovemaking had been gentle—not just because of Piper's injury, but because of the vulnerability Jake sensed in her following her recent experiences. He sensed her need for optimism, and so he offered her something that had been firmly on his mind the past few days.

He turned on his side to face her. "This ... *you* ... it's the only good thing that has happened to me for as long as I can remember."

She remained on her back; her injury prevented her from turning. "You already know how I feel about you."

"I'll be honest, Piper. I really don't know how *my* situation will play out back home, but I want to make a good go of this with you."

"Glad to hear it!"

"No, Piper, *seriously*. You ... *this* ... I've not felt this way in so long."

She reached to take his hand.

"But I come with baggage."

"I know."

"*Serious* baggage."

Piper let her head fall to the side so she could meet his

eyes. "That's been fairly obvious since I saw the lone British man skulking away in the far corner of the Taps."

"It's much more than that." Jake sighed. "Piper ... I've killed people."

Piper turned her head to face the ceiling.

He gave her a moment to digest his words.

"You were a policeman."

"Yes, but I didn't kill these people in the line of duty."

Piper gulped. "Were they innocent people?"

"No ... but does that excuse it?"

"It depends, I guess, on whether you had a choice."

"I had no choice in those *actual* moments, but the situations I placed myself in? Yes, I had a choice of being where I was." He explained his involvement with the organised crime syndicate, Article SE, and the favors he could offer them in his role as a detective sergeant for the Wiltshire Police. "Small things, at first. Just to earn extra money for my son, for his future, but things quickly got out of hand." He told her about how he had killed Borya Turgenev, a Russian assassin, working on behalf of Article SE. "But it was him or my closest friend and his wife."

"And your closest friend was a good man?"

"The best."

"And this Borya was a bad man."

Jake snorted. "The worst."

"So, again, what choice did you have?"

Jake took a deep breath. "There was a young boy ..." He paused. He couldn't find the words to continue.

Piper let her head fall to the side again.

He couldn't look her in the eyes, so he turned to stare at the ceiling. He felt a tear run down his cheek.

"You don't have to talk about—"

"Paul Conway."

"Okay ..."

"His name was Paul Conway. And his death is my fault." He rubbed at his eyes with his thumb and forefinger. "I was watching an ex-Russian spy. I was feeding Article SE details of his movements. They put a bomb in his car."

"Did you know they wanted to kill him?"

Jake looked at her. The answer was too obvious to give airtime.

"So, what happened to the boy?"

"Paul. He lived next door. He was playing badminton with his brother. The shuttlecock went into the ex-spy's driveway while he was getting into his car. Fuck, Piper, I *watched* it happen."

She stroked his face.

"I held him in my arms."

She leaned in and pressed her forehead against his.

"I left him on the road. I ran. I never had chance to tell his parents how sorry I was." He cried for a time. The horrendous experience stayed with him every waking minute. This was the first time he'd shared it. The relief, although bittersweet, was welcomed. Once he had regained enough control, he said, "I told them I was out. Obviously. I wanted nothing more to do with Article SE."

"You did the right thing."

"Except ... it doesn't really work like that. You don't just tell Article SE you're done."

"What does that mean?"

Jake shrugged. "It means I'm *here* with you."

"I don't follow."

"Well, if I stayed in England, I'd be dead already. I needed a place as far from home as possible. I had an American passport. My ancestors were from round here. It all seemed to fall into place."

26

"But your family. Your boy, Frank. Your ex-wife ... Are they safe?"

"Yes. The closest friend I told you about before? He has my back in that regard. Besides, it's not in Article SE's style to move on an innocent family in Salisbury. Imagine the publicity. No, they will be patient. They will see me as a dead man walking. It doesn't matter if it's tomorrow or in thirty years, they will even their scales. They aren't an emotional bunch. They tend to act methodically. Are you okay?"

Piper kissed his forehead. "It's a lot to take in, admittedly, but I'm so glad you're telling me the truth."

"I love you, and I'd understand if you wanted to walk away. The things I've done. Do you really want to be with someone like that?"

"This is *not* who you are though. Not really."

"I'm a big believer that what you've done defines you."

"That's because you're a cop. Me? I believe in second chances."

Jake shook his head. "I'm not sure if I deserve a second—"

"Have you completely forgotten about our conversation earlier? Amber? Her illness?"

"This is different. I made choices. Rational choices. I cannot claim diminished responsibility!"

"Not true. Your marriage broke down. A dangerous ex-girlfriend threatened you. All these things can force us to make the wrong decisions. You can make amends. You *are* making amends."

Is making amends killing your biological father, Piper? He opened his mouth to release the truth but decided against it. He didn't want to put her through any more

27

anguish today. "Being with you is more than a second chance. It's like winning the bloody lottery."

She kissed him. "Well, enjoy your winnings."

He smiled. "I am doing. Too much."

"Did you mean what you said, Jake? Are we really making a go of this?"

"I think so. I am telling you all of my secrets, after all."

"Are you safe here, with me, in Blue Falls?"

"Yes. Even those closest to me back home don't know where I am. They can't find me here."

"Well, Blue Falls is the middle of nowhere."

"Precisely. That's why I chose it."

Alpheus Bird wheeled the chair closer to his desktop computer. He nibbled his bottom lip, enough to cause pain but not enough to draw blood. He liked *feeling* pain almost as much as he liked inflicting it. But blood? He never wanted to taste his own, only that of his prey.

He eyed the video camera on a tripod, angled toward a futon. No expense had been spared on that camera. State-of-the-art. His last kill had paid very well indeed. He surveyed the sagging ceiling and the blistered wallpaper. He could upgrade from this hovel to something special if he really wanted to, but he liked flying below the radar.

He watched the paused home movie on the desktop screen featuring him standing with his back close to the camera, obscuring his visitor and the bed she lay upon. Starting at his muscular shoulders, Alpheus traced sharpened fingernails over the large red-tailed hawk tattoo. Its wingspan concealed his entire back. He nibbled hard enough for a burst of pain but not hard enough to break skin.

On the video, Alpheus strode forward naked; sitting, he now admired his formidable thighs and his sinewy calves, then he appreciated the beauty of the naked woman who lay face down on the futon. He'd employed her from the same place he'd employed all the others, but this one was a true gem. There wasn't an ounce of fat on her, and she pushed her toned backside high in the air as she reached under herself and moaned pleasurably.

Alpheus watched himself mount her from behind. She welcomed it. He watched his eyes roll on the video as he moved inside her—gentle, at first. Now, watching, he felt again the same pleasure in his loins.

On the home movie, the gentle start ended as the heavy thrusting began. The woman showed no resistance or surprise. She would have been warned at her agency. She'd known what she was signing up for.

Now, Alpheus gripped the edges of his desk. He did this to prevent his hands from moving to his crotch to experience again that pleasure from earlier. Masturbation disgusted him. He prided himself on being a wild animal that took what it needed and didn't have to retreat into the solace of self-pleasure—a domain that spoke strongly of failure. Would a hawk fail in its ability to find a mate? Fail to take what it wanted?

He looked at his bloodstained fingernails. All but two of the sharpened points had survived the encounter, which was good going.

When he heard the woman scream, his eyes flicked back up. On the screen, he'd already leaned forward and pinned her flat under his large body. He was digging his makeshift talons into her upper arms as he drove himself hard inside her. Again and again.

He'd positioned the camera too far away for him to see the blood running down her arms, but he remembered it well. He nibbled his lip slightly harder while restraining his wandering hands by gripping the table.

He was just wondering if those two sharpened nails had broken off inside her arms when his email pinged. He paused the video and opened the message. After reading it, he deleted the correspondence and went to the front door of his one-room apartment. He opened the door, leaned out, looked both ways down the empty corridor, then picked up the box on the floor.

As he sauntered back to his desktop, he opened the box and removed a small clamshell phone. He threw the cardboard in a trashcan under his desk, placed the burner beside the keyboard, then hit Play on the video. He watched the red hawk on his back flex its wings. She was now pleading, as they always did—eventually.

Yet, they kept coming back. Money, especially in the high amounts he offered, could be a very persuasive thing.

The phone rang. He muted the video but kept watching. In the movie, his prey had completely submitted, and he was close to climax.

He flipped the phone.

"Mr. Bird." It was a British accent.

"Yes."

"My name is Walter."

The woman in the video had turned her head and stared at the camera. Her eyes were wide, and her face contorted.

"I know who you are. You work for them."

"In a fashion. So, you understand the importance of this phone call?"

"Yes."

"I need you to do something," Walter said.

On the video, his earlier self climaxed. He yanked his head back. His eyes and mouth were wide. Alpheus smiled. "If you need me to hunt and you need me to kill, then I'm listening."

3

"I BARELY RECOGNIZE you," Jake said, climbing into the passenger seat of Officer Lillian Sanborn's car.

"Fancied a change," she said, running a hand through her hair.

"Blonde to brunette though. Don't people usually go the other way?"

"I don't know. I'm waiting on the results of the survey."

Jake laughed. "Anyway, to what do I owe the pleasure? I've never known of anyone so desperate to take me for a coffee! It's life-affirming."

Lillian reversed out of the driveway of Piper's family home. "Not a social visit, I'm afraid."

"I guessed as much"—Jake buckled his seatbelt—"being that you haven't returned any of my calls in the last four days."

"Been busy looking for the chief and Kayla. I'm in touch now, aren't I?" Lillian straightened the vehicle on the main road.

"Yes, strange that, as last time I saw you, you were mouthpiece for Louise warning me off the hunt."

Lieutenant Louise Price worked for the Maine State Police. Following the discovery of Gabriel's sister's body a week back, she'd practically taken over Blue Falls Police Department. A task made easier by the fact that the local chief of police, Gabriel Jewell, was currently on the run for both murder and kidnapping.

Jake thought of Piper lying naked back in her bedroom. "So, why have you interrupted my siesta, Lillian?"

Lillian smiled. "The lieutenant wants to see you."

"Come again?"

"You heard."

Jake shook his head. "She must be trying to get me deported or something."

"It's to do with Kayla and the chief. She wants your help."

"I don't believe it."

"The Lord works in mysterious ways."

"There's mysterious, and then there's ridiculous. What does she want?"

Lillian shrugged. "I don't actually know, but she was pretty adamant that I get you to her immediately."

"Well that certainly has got me curious." Jake smiled at Lillian. "Admit it. You did want to see me though, really; didn't you?"

"What makes you say that?"

"You picked me up. Why not just tell me to drive in?"

"Don't flatter yourself, buster. I came in case you did a runner."

"A runner? From Blue Falls? Why would I do that? There isn't a more beautiful and tranquil spot in the world."

"Stop at beautiful! I'd buy that. You lost me at tranquil."

"So, if the lieutenant is going to see me anyway, Lil, how about filling me in on the investigation to date."

Lillian indicated left off a rotary, smiling. "Can you see now why I haven't been returning your calls?"

"The relentless pressure?" Jake raised an eyebrow.

"Something along those lines. Look, Jake, truth be told, there isn't much to report. We've been door to door in Rosstown. We sifted through so much surveillance footage I felt like I was going blind. We've blocked the interstate. Seriously, Jake, at the point you lost him on the bridge, he disappeared into the ether."

"That sounds like good news to me."

Lillian pulled over opposite the steps leading to the police department. She killed the engine and flashed him a confused look. "How so?"

"You've just told me he's still local. The fact you haven't found him yet had me worried that he'd left the country."

Lillian nodded. "I'll take you to the lieutenant."

"The ice queen?" Jake shivered.

"She's not that bad when you get to know her."

"Wouldn't know, she's not exactly opened that door to me, with her constant looks of disgust."

Lillian opened the door.

Jake put his hand on her shoulder. "I didn't just call to hound you about the case, you know."

Lillian sighed. "I know."

"How *are* you, Lil?"

"I'm okay."

"I hoped you could talk about it with me, if you needed to."

"I'm fine, honestly."

"You lost someone, Lillian."

"I only knew Ewan a couple of days. I'm hardly sure it counts as a loss."

Jake looked deep into her eyes. "It does, Lil. It really does."

And the way your boss murdered the Maine State Trooper is a hard loss to bear. "Answer my calls, Lil. Please."

Lillian smiled. "Will do, Jake."

Even though this wasn't the first time Jake had been inside the Blue Falls Police Department, it might as well have been, because the place suddenly felt so different. He recalled the caterwauling on his first visit when the male officers, with attitudes wedged way back in the first half of last century, had hounded Lillian, their only female colleague. Witnessing that zoo in full flow had angered Jake, and to see it under control elevated his respect for Lieutenant Louise Price.

In fact, when she opened her office door and greeted him, he told her so. "Well done on taming the jungle."

"You can congratulate me when I'm finished, because, in case you'd forgotten, the lion is still out there." She went to sit behind her desk.

Jake was glad to see she'd taken down that horrendous picture of Gabriel's father, ex-Chief of Police Earl Jewell— another rampaging bigot.

"He's no king of the jungle, believe me," Jake said, sitting down. "He lacks courage and strength, and last time I saw him, he was out of control, wired up to the eyeballs on Adderall."

The tall, black lieutenant leaned back in her chair. She caught the direct glow of the lamp overhead, and her dark hair, jammed into a bun, shone. She clamped her hands together, then pointed at him with her two forefingers pressed together. "You'd know, I guess, Mr. Pettman, being that you spent so much time with him."

"And what's that supposed to mean?"

"I think it's fairly obvious what I mean."

Jake shook his head. "If that's why you asked me here, Lieutenant, you're barking up the wrong tree. There is no love lost between me and Gabriel. I was forced to watch him gun down Priscilla Stone and three others, including your officer, while handcuffed to a radiator. Have you forgotten that?"

"Ewan was a good man. Believe me, I've not forgotten anything about that day. Neither have I forgotten that *you*" —she pointed at him again—"went to the Stone residence with him."

"Yes, following a tip from one of your officers while you were busy rummaging through the wreckage of an explosion! I was only trying to help."

"By taking a dangerous man with you?"

"I concede that was a bad move, but, in my defence, he was still chief of police. I thought he'd see the light."

"You thought wrong, and now he's God-knows-where with a fourteen-year-old girl in tow."

Jake shrugged. "And you think I've an idea of where he is? Well, I heard you were getting desperate, but you are really scraping the barrel. I've spent most of my life helping people. If I had an inkling of where that young girl was, we wouldn't even be sitting here—"

"Stop." She held up a hand to silence him. "That is not why you're here." She focused on a picture on her desk and stroked the top of the frame.

Jake couldn't see the picture but assumed it was of her family. He recalled the story Lillian had told him. One evening, six years ago, Louise had come home from work to find her husband and three daughters missing—no evidence of forced entry, no traces of intruders, and the husband's vehicle was still in the driveway. Her family hadn't been seen since.

She looked up. "Let's talk about the Bickfords."

"Jesus!" Jake leaned back in his chair. "Don't you bloody start."

"You misunderstand, Mr. Pettman. I don't bring up your ancestors as a form of judgement over you, which, seeing your reaction, is something you have experienced a lot since arriving at Blue Falls. I bring them up because they're part of this town's history."

Jake sighed. "Well, you're probably speaking to the wrong person about the Bickfords. Apart from the fact they allowed me easy access to a passport, I don't know a great deal about them. I imagine, at this stage, you probably know more."

"Tell me what know about them."

"Shouldn't you be looking for Kayla and Gabriel?"

"Humor me."

Jake leaned forward. "They ran Blue Falls Taps as a brothel in the nineteenth century. They stole children from local, more impoverished towns. It's a despicable story. I didn't care to look into it much further."

"Do you know what happened to the vile lot?"

"They were run from town and fled to England, hence" —he pointed at himself—"they have descendants. But you should know I'm nothing like them. The line has been well and truly diluted since then. I'd love to say *purified*, but, of course, I'm not perfect."

"No one is. Did you know they killed some of those children?"

"Five, I believe. They found two at Lookout Corner. A final *fuck you* to the town."

Louise nodded. "Yes. There're still Bickfords dotted around Maine and Vermont. Did you know that?"

"Sort of. Haven't given it much thought. They'd be stupid to return here, wouldn't they?"

Louise raised an eyebrow. "You came back."

"Not a Bickford, sorry. I renounced that name. And, without a blood test, I'm never conceding to a genetic link. So, unless you're springing a surprise on me, the Bickfords are long gone from Blue Falls."

Louise's eyebrow remained raised.

"You're about to spring a surprise on me, aren't you?"

She stood, paced to the side of the desk, and leaned against it.

Jake remained seated. Due to his height, he wasn't a man used to being towered over, but the opening of Louise's revelation had him rooted to the chair.

"As you rightly pointed out, during your grand entrance before, our search has stalled somewhat. Delving into Gabriel's history these past days seemed a viable option in trying to locate him."

"And he's connected to the Bickfords, *how?*"

"You sound shocked. I've been in many small towns such as this one. Their foundations are often comprised of secrets, and nothing shocks me anymore."

"I'm all ears."

Louise paced behind Jake. "As you pointed out, the Bickfords fled the scene of the crime. That was in eighteen sixty. The Blue Falls Taps took up new ownership under auction. During the next thirty years, that little watering hole changed ownership six times! It was actually lost to new owners *twice* in card games." Having passed Jake,

Louise now leaned on the other side of the desk. "In eighteen ninety-one, a young, married couple came into town and bought the Taps." Louise returned to her seat and opened a drawer. She placed a grainy daguerreotype on the table in front of Jake.

He studied the two adults and three older children, all smartly dressed for the photograph, in white shirts and black braces, apart from the mother, who wore a checkered blouse.

"The Bickfords circa eighteen sixties, just before they fled. Note the large, chiselled faces and diminutive noses on the father and his two elder boys. Similar to you, I might add."

Jake looked up. "Don't see it myself."

She took another photograph from the drawer and threw it down in front of Jake. The picture quality was clearer. The couple on it looked barely out of their teens. "Dated eighteen ninety-two. Fern and Luca Holbrook. The couple who bought the Taps. What do you notice?"

He stared at Luca's face—large, chiselled with a diminutive nose. "This is your evidence then that the Bickfords returned and bought the Taps. A *nose?*"

Louise shrugged. "The family resemblance is striking, you must admit."

Jake nodded, then noticed Fern also had the same resemblance. "These look more like brother and sister than a married couple."

"Agreed. They might have been masquerading as a couple, or—"

"A serious case of incest is going on in the family."

Louise nodded.

Jake felt his stomach turn. He recalled his earlier words to Louise. *"Without a blood test, I'm never conceding to a genetic link."* Jake shook his head. "I don't buy it. They were public enemy number one! Thirty years is not that long. People don't forget that quickly."

Louise smiled. "I agree. I met it with the same scepticism, but then I found this." She reached into the drawer yet again and removed a photocopy of an old newspaper cutting.

Jake scanned the article. In 1931, both Fern and Luca Holbrook were murdered in their own home due to a botched robbery. The thieves were apprehended, and a significant amount of jewellery was recovered. Jake's blood froze when he reached the final paragraph. Some of the jewellery had been engraved with the name, *Bickford.*

When Jake made eye contact with Louise, he wondered if he looked as sick as he felt. "Maybe the Bickfords left some jewellery in the Taps when they fled Blue Falls, and the Holbrooks decided to keep it?"

"Maybe. That's what the journalist who wrote that article believed. But ..." She slid over another photocopy of an old newspaper article, much longer than the other.

Jake started to read.

"I'll save you time. That article discloses the identity of the two murderous thieves."

Jake looked up from the article into Louise's eyes. "You're about to tell me it wasn't a botched robbery, aren't you?"

Louise nodded. "The thieves both carried the surname Hall. Seventy years earlier, in eighteen fifty-nine, a girl by the name of Muriel Hall disappeared. In eighteen sixty, following the Bickford's escape, she was one of the dead children found at Lookout Point."

"So, the descendants of the Halls murdered the

descendants of the Bickfords. A grudge passed down a family tree. Maybe I should be watching my back?"

"I imagine you already are."

Jake smirked. "Always." He stared at the material Louise had slid over the desk to him and thought about the tale. "Why do you think the Halls waited so long for payback? The Holbrooks were here running the Taps for almost forty years!"

"I'm guessing the Holbrooks kept their secret well-hidden for a very long time."

"Until?"

Louise shrugged. "I don't know. Somehow, they must have let the cat out of the bag. Reports indicate that Luca was a drunken cardplayer. I suspect he ran his mouth off one night, potentially boasting about his infamous heritage. Maybe one of the Hall's descendants was at that card table. Maybe someone close to the Hall family was. Either way, letting that secret slip cost Luca and Fern Holbrook their lives."

"Okay, you're starting to convince me, but if the Holbrooks are already dead, where's this story going? I thought you were going to reveal that the Bickfords—myself not included, of course—were still in town?"

"Luca and Fern Holbrook had a son who survived the botched robbery. The Taps stayed in that family right up until present day."

"So, the Holbrooks—or the Bickfords, as you suspect —*still* own the taps."

Louise nodded. "They do. Ethan and Willow Holbrook. Early forties."

"But *surely* those thieves, the Halls, eventually revealed that the Holbrooks were really Bickfords?"

Louise shook her head. "Seems not. Despite killing Fern and Luca Holbrook, the Halls did not reveal their secret identities to Blue Falls. Who knows why? Maybe they considered justice served and didn't want to ruin the life of that orphaned boy. Maybe someone connected to, or even related to, the Bickfords threatened them in jail. I really couldn't tell you. The point of all this is, Mr. Pettman, that the Bickfords, your bloodline, are still in Blue Falls, running the taps."

"Jesus. I wonder if Ethan and Willow even know they're Bickfords!"

Louise leaned back in her chair and smiled. "That's where you come in. I need you to find out for me."

Jake shook his head, confused. "But why? What has this got to do with Gabriel and Kayla?"

"A number of years back, Ethan and Willow had dealings with Gabriel."

Jake leaned forward in his chair again. "I'm listening."

"Gabriel was investigating them for some unknown reason."

"Unknown?"

"The files, computer-based, have been corrupted."

"Intentionally, perhaps?"

She shrugged. "You know him better than I do. Why do you think this *mysterious* investigation died?"

"Maybe he found out they were descended from the Bickfords?"

"Seems reasonable. And maybe they paid him to bury the truth."

Jake nodded. "I see. So, you're thinking this is a lead to Gabriel?"

"I'm thinking this is the only lead we have so far; whether it actually leads to him is a whole different matter entirely. I need your help in finding out."

"Why?"

"Think about it. If Ethan and Willow know they are descended from the Bickfords, and a Lieutenant from the MSP marches in to ask them if this is the case, they may clam up. They do good business at the Taps; I'm not sure they want to jeopardize that by linking themselves to child-killers. But, if a relative walks in"—she pointed at him—"and tugs at their heart strings, then who knows? Maybe it'll all come out, including the truth about what happened with Gabriel."

"Sounds like a long shot."

"Our only shot."

"And if they are descended from Bickfords? And they are walking around under the same black cloud as me, then what? Are you planning to expose them and ruin them?"

"Do you care, Mr. Pettman?"

"Actually, yes I do. Very much."

"In that case, you have my word. They won't be exposed." She stroked the top of the frame. "The only thing that matters to us all is the missing girl."

4

AFTER WASHING THE blood from beneath his fingernails, Alpheus slipped on his loose leather gloves; letting the eyes of others wander over those sharpened points was just asking for trouble. In the bathroom mirror, he admired the defined shape of his upper body, which was accentuated by a tight, white short-sleeved shirt.

He opened the bathroom cabinet and reached in for his most sentimental possession. His stomach twisted. Gone.

He touched his upper chest; it felt naked without his mother's pendant. His breathing quickened. He checked the top shelf and closed the cabinet. In the mirror, he could see the futon in the other room. The dishevelled sheets sent his mind to the hooker he'd paid handsomely for discretion.

She'd stolen it.

Taking the pendant, which carried a photo of mother and young son together, was an act not befitting hawk prey. And it spoke loudly of Alpheus's *own* failure. He closed his eyes and imagined the red-tailed hawk. With its long wings, it could soar high on those thermals for long periods of time, intimidating its prey, sending them into a terrified frenzy. The target would waste its valuable energy trying to flee, its senses and fight dampening to the point of collapse.

The hawk soared.

Waited.

Screaming its intentions.

So, when the prey knew nothing but anguish and the hawk felt nothing but true superiority, then came the swoop.

Alpheus opened his eyes. He stared into his own pupils, quickly tilted his head, and heard the crack of his neck. It seems today he'd swooped *too* soon. He narrowed his eyes and turned from the bathroom mirror.

Next time he swooped, he would ensure the prey knew its place and understood its fate.

It was immediately clear that Ethan and Willow Holbrook were hiding something.

Ethan Holbrook grunted his greeting while his wife, Willow, led Jake into their kitchen. Despite Jake then asking him how he was doing, Ethan did not follow up his grunt with any dialogue. Instead, he just slammed cards down on the table as he played a version of solitaire that Jake was unfamiliar with. Every now and again, he paused to stroke his long beard as he contemplated his next move.

Jake considered asking him if he was a man of few words, or simply a man who was opting to be ignorant with a guest in his kitchen, but sensibly decided against poking a bee in its own hive.

"Would you like coffee?" Willow asked, pulling a chair from under the kitchen table for Jake to sit.

"No thanks, ma'am. Drinking coffee in the afternoon turns me into a night owl."

"Same," Willow said. "It also plays havoc with my anxiety levels."

Ethan slammed down another card.

Willow watched him sheepishly. "Sorry, Mr. Pettman, my husband hates it when I talk about personal issues."

Better than not talking at all. Jake glanced at Ethan, who had not yet acknowledged his visitor. "No need to apologize, ma'am. And call me Jake."

"If you call me Willow." She smiled.

"Okay, Willow." Jake shook her hand. She didn't bear the same Bickford family resemblance. She had a wiry body and the thin, gaunt face that often came with the excessively anxious. It was familiar to Jake, as his own mother had been particularly neurotic before the heart attack that had taken her so young.

"Please sit, Jake," Willow said.

Jake sat on the opposite side of the kitchen table from Ethan. He observed the ignorant, burly man, who did possess the same Bickford family look—the chiselled face and the diminutive nose.

"I have to admit I just told a lie on your doorstep, Willow," Jake said.

Her smile fell away, and her eyes darted from left to right. "You're not here about the job?"

"No. I'm afraid not." His heart quickened. The last thing that he wanted to do was give her a panic attack. "But I need you to know I don't come intending any harm."

Ethan slammed down another card.

Jake felt his temperature rise. He bit his bottom lip to stop himself firing off a comment that may result in a nasty confrontation. "You know I'm descended from the

Bickfords. I made no secret of it when I came into town. I wasn't fully aware of the family history, so I didn't think it—"

Ethan brushed most of the cards onto the floor and guffawed. "You don't come meaning harm, eh?"

"That's what I said, Mr. Holbrook. I'm here—"

"Out of the goodness of your heart?" Ethan rose to his feet. "To meet and greet the locals?"

Jake bit his lip again.

"Go on, Mr. Pettman. Do tell us the purpose of your visit to our home today. What delightful conversation can we look forward to?"

"I came to find out if we're related."

"Ha!" Ethan flicked his hand back and forth between them. "You think we look alike!"

Jake shook his head. *Not with that ridiculous beard, my friend.*

"I think you should leave now, Mr. Pettman," Willow said. "I really shouldn't have let you in. You lied to me, and now my husband is getting really angry."

Ethan picked up the chair by its back and threw it against the wall behind him. The chair didn't break, but Jake could see the dent it made in the wall. "I'm not angry. Not yet. This is me being rather calm, but unless you—"

Jake stood. "Right, *okay,* enough! Let's cut this bravado, Ethan. I was a policeman back where I came from, so hostile responses to my presence are nothing new to me. Ignoring me while you play solitaire and throwing a chair is not having the impact you think it's having. I haven't slipped an inch from my comfort zone. So, the best thing for you to do is just hear me out, park the fury, and acknowledge that I genuinely mean you no harm."

Ethan turned his back to Jake and wandered to the wall.

He ran his fingers over the fresh dent. "No harm? How could you possibly believe the conversation we are about to have could cause no harm?"

"You have my word, Ethan. You and Willow both. Whatever happens from this moment forth, I have your back. I don't take my promises lightly. You're descended from the Bickfords, aren't you?"

Ethan turned. "Obviously. It's the reason you're here, isn't it? And despite being descended from despicable men, I'm an upstanding member of society, running a successful business, and taking good care of my wife and daughter. So, can you see why this conversation might antagonise somewhat?"

"Is your daughter home?"

"No," Willow said. "Molly is twenty-five. She lives in Sharon's Edge."

"Does she know about her heritage?"

Ethan nodded. "We had no choice but to tell her. Someone put us in a very difficult fucking situation a while back. Actually, it's very similar to the one you're putting us in right now. What's your endgame?"

"Not the same as Gabriel Jewell's."

Ethan flinched and put his fist to his mouth.

Willow took several steps backward until she was standing by the kitchen sink.

"You know, then?" Ethan asked.

"Suspected, but I didn't know. In fact, I still don't know a great deal. I really need you to help with that."

"It's not a nice tale."

"If it involves Gabriel Jewell, I expect it isn't."

"I thought our secret was safe," Ethan said. "Before I tell you anything, I want you to explain how you ended up here."

"Okay. Let's sit. It's better with calm tempers. And I've changed my mind, Willow; I will take a coffee. Who has time for sleep anyway?"

"I'll join you," Willow said. "After all, I'm already anxious."

Jake talked his way through the discoveries Louise had made regarding the murder of Fern and Luca Holbrook.

"She wasn't the first person to make these connections," Ethan said. "And, unfortunately, she won't be the last. I've always felt that we were living on borrowed time."

"I'm sorry," Jake said. "I really am. You don't deserve to have your lives turned upside down based on something your ancestors did. I'm pretty sure most people could find some pretty heinous things way back in their family tree if they looked hard enough."

"We always planned to keep Molly in the dark about the Bickfords. We hoped one day the history would just fizzle out. Our secret ceases to be a secret if no one knows about it. Wishful thinking, eh? Gabriel Jewell put an end to that when he turned up on our doorstep."

"What did he want?"

"To investigate the claim that we were running drugs from the Blue Fall Taps."

"And were you?"

"No! Of course not!" Willow said.

"We have a good business here," Ethan said. "Why sully it with drugs? Jotham MacLeoid had tried, on several occasions, to convince us to allow it to go on in the dark corners of our establishment, and every time, we knocked it back. Yes, he threatened to drive us out of

49

business if we didn't comply, but it never really came to anything."

"He was too busy trying to take over the world," Willow said.

"Yes," Ethan said, "I guess we're very small fry compared to the empire he was building."

Building, Jake thought, taking a mouthful of coffee. *I put an end to that.* "Could it have been Jotham who got Gabriel Jewell to put pressure on you with the threat of investigation?"

"That's what we thought at first." Ethan studied a playing card he turned over and over. "That would have been preferable."

"What did he want?" Jake said.

Ethan crumpled the playing card in his palm by making a fist. "Something worse. Something sinister." He looked up at something on the wall behind Jake.

Jake turned and traced his line of sight to a framed photograph of a young girl in a school uniform with fiery-red hair wrapped into two long, tight ponytails. Jake turned back to look at Ethan, who was now giving his beard small, sharp tugs, causing his head to bob. "Your daughter?"

Ethan didn't respond; instead, he gave himself another couple of sharp yanks.

Willow approached her husband and put her hand on his shoulder. "Honey?"

Ethan's hand fell from his beard, and he regarded his wife with tearful eyes.

She responded with a tear sliding down her cheek.

"I'm not here with the same agenda as *that* man," Jake said.

Ethan glared at him. "I know that. If you were, you'd be

already bleeding out in the corner of the room, but this doesn't make it any less dangerous."

"Please tell me what happened."

"Before I tell you this, it is important for you to understand something."

"I'm listening."

"If something happens to our Molly because of what is said in this room today, then we won't have anything left to live for." He glared at Jake. "And neither will you."

Jake nodded. "Understood, but believe me, nothing will happen to Molly, because my intention is to stop Gabriel Jewell."

"Okay then." He looked at Willow. "Do you want to leave?"

Willow retracted her hand from his shoulder. "No! And fuck you for suggesting it!"

"I didn't mean to offend. I just didn't think it was necessary for us both to relive it."

"I relive it every fucking day, Ethan."

Ethan sighed and faced Jake. "Gabriel Jewell came to our door, having made those same connections. We may be descended from the Bickfords, but we are *not* Bickfords. You need to understand that subtle difference."

"I do. I feel exactly the same way; in fact, I would argue the difference isn't even *subtle*."

"Good. So, let's not pretend we're related; we aren't and never will be. The Bickfords are from a whole different world."

"I hear you."

Ethan leaned over the table and slid out another chair from beneath the table. He nodded at his wife to sit.

She obliged.

"Chief Jewell threatened to expose us as drug dealers,

and then expose our family names. That combination would have destroyed our business. I'm also pretty sure that if the locals didn't burn down the place, with us inside it of course, they'd have run us out of town, penniless."

Jake shook his head. "I'm sorry he put you through that."

"And then he gave us his terms of silence."

Jake looked down at the table. He could suddenly feel the eyes of the red-headed girl in the photograph boring into him. The impending revelation was all too obvious. And heinous.

"He asked for our fourteen-year-old daughter."

Jake took a sharp inhalation through his nose. He looked up and made eye contact with Ethan. He wondered if he should promise Ethan that he would kill the monster when he finally found him, and then wondered if he would enjoy such a promise. He kept the words inside.

Ethan held a finger in the air. "Understand this though. He never had sex with her. That was *never* on the table. He claimed that wasn't what he wanted. I told him that if he laid a finger on her, I would burn down the Taps myself, with me and him inside it, and Molly and Willow would go somewhere new to start again." He waved his finger. "*Understand that*, Mr. Pettman. I never pimped my daughter. Death would have been the first option in that case."

"I understand."

"He only wanted to spend time with her. Read to her. Talk to her. He said Molly reminded him of his sister Collette. His sister had disappeared when she was fourteen —same age as my daughter."

And there, clear as day, was the connection to Kayla MacLeoid. In these young girls, he must find reminders of the beloved sister he'd lost when he was a young man. Jake recalled some of Jotham Macleoid's final words as he had taunted Gabriel: *"Remember those young girls at Sharon's Edge?"* Jake felt hope gestating within him. *Did this mean he wasn't sexually abusing these children? Did it mean he revered them? Could Kayla MacLeoid be found unharmed?*

"I told him," Ethan continued, "that this would only happen under supervision. At first, he accepted this, but"— he wiped away a tear, then took his wife's hand—"over time, he pushed harder and harder until we allowed him some time alone with her."

Willow stroked her husband's hand, comforting him as he struggled to continue. "It wasn't my husband's fault, Jake; you must understand. It happened so slowly. He just pushed harder and harder, until—"

Ethan slammed his fist on the table. "He *never* had sex with her. *Know* that. If he had, we would know. She *would* have told us."

Jake nodded. "I believe you."

"But it did get worse ... to my almighty shame, it got worse." He tugged his beard again. "She came to us one day and told us that he was now holding her hand as he read to her."

Jake clenched his hands together in front of his coffee cup.

"*At first* she was okay with it," Willow said. "She said he was nice, gentle, that he didn't mean any harm."

Jake nodded. *At first ... at first ...*

"But then the bastard would put his head in her lap and ask her to stroke his hair." Ethan stood up. "Like he was some kind of fucking baby!"

While Willow stared at the table, Ethan paced back and forth, head down, deep in thought.

After a sustained period of silence, Jake felt no option but to press them further. "And then?"

Ethan stopped pacing and faced Jake. "Then?" A ghost of a smile flicked across his face. "Then, I beat the living shit out of him."

"And how did he respond?"

"Believe it or not, with composure. He simply reissued the threat. He'd been reading to her for over nine months, and she was now fifteen. He warned me that it was impossible for him to stop now, that if he had to force the issue, he would do, and that would end badly for all concerned." He started to pace again.

"So?"

"So? I locked the fucking front door and called his bluff."

"And he wasn't bluffing, was he?"

"No. He got the police to raid us that night. Of course, they found nothing, but it was a warning. The anxiety over watching those officers tearing the Taps, *our home*, apart devastated my daughter. Molly came to me the next day and said I should let her continue to visit Gabriel. I refused, of course, but both her and that twisted bastard's constant threats ground me down eventually." Ethan took a deep breath, then stared at the picture of his daughter, sorrow etched on his face.

"And this continued until she was sixteen," Willow said. "Until she was too old and he grew bored of her."

Jake sat back in his chair. "Why?"

"He didn't explain himself. He just said he no longer needed to see us, that we could now move on with our lives." Ethan chortled. "Very courteous of him."

"And has he stayed away all this time?"

"Yes," Willow said. "He stayed true to his word. He was finished. But ..." She gagged on a sudden onslaught of tears.

"*But* ..." Ethan put his fists on the table and leaned forward. "The damage was done."

"This must have been traumatic—"

"*No.* You misunderstand. There was more."

"You said he was finished."

"Yes, he was finished, but that didn't mean it was over. More happened on those visits than we knew about ... until years later, when Molly, bless her, was suffering from PTSD. Then the truth came out. Do you really want to know what he did?"

The rational part of Jake was screaming at him to remain in ignorance. He already knew what his next move was now, and the additional details of Gabriel's abuse wouldn't alter that in the slightest. But the natural part of Jake, the *curious* part of Jake, the part of Jake that desired truth, won out in the end. "Yes."

"After the visits started again, he would masturbate in front of her."

Jake's stomach turned.

"But you must understand; we never knew. *We never knew.* If Molly had told us, I would have stopped it—strike that, I *would* have killed him."

Jake turned back to look at the photograph of Molly in her school uniform. *Poor girl.* Jake tried to hold his tongue, but he succumbed to a sudden surge of anger. "You should have gone to the police and exposed him. A man like that shouldn't have been allowed to continue."

"He *is* the police," Ethan said.

Jake tried his best to expel the anger from his facial expression and his tone of voice. Condemning the Holbrook couple now would serve no purpose. He struggled. "There are ways. You could have got in touch with the state police!"

"Gabriel would have ruined us."

Hasn't he already ruined you? "And how about the people he has ruined since then?"

"I don't know anything about that."

But you wouldn't now, would you? You have opted for ignorance. "You know he is missing, don't you?"

"Yes. Good riddance."

"He took a fourteen-year-old girl with him."

"Good God," Willow said, putting her hand to her mouth.

Jake nodded. "Yes. He should have been stopped. This *could* have been avoided."

Ethan pointed at Jake. "Don't you stand in judgement over us! You don't know how we've suffered ... how my daughter has suffered."

"I won't stand in judgement, Ethan, not if you help me now, when another fourteen-year-old girl needs us."

"Who is the young girl?" Willow asked, wiping at her eyes.

"I can't tell you that. Please tell me when the last time either of you spoke to Molly was?"

They both looked at each other.

"Why?" Ethan asked.

"How long?"

"Late last week," Willow said.

"Phone her," Jake said. "Call her now."

"You don't think ...?" Willow asked.

"I don't know anything right now," Jake said. "But Gabriel Jewell is a desperate man. A *cornered* desperate man. If he's still not been found, someone must be helping him."

"Molly wouldn't do that," Willow said.

Not by choice. "Please. Call her. Gabriel doesn't have many people to run to. Unfortunately, your daughter's history with him makes her one of the possibilities."

"This is bullshit," Ethan said.

Jake watched Ethan as he called Molly, watched him as he waited for her to answer, watched him as he left her a message, watched his face pale.

He placed the cellphone on the kitchen table. "She must be busy."

"She *always* picks up," Willow said.

Ethan turned to his wife. "She *must* be busy."

"There is no need to panic," Jake said. "But if you give me her address, I'd like to go there and put everyone's mind at rest."

5

"IS DOLORES YOUR real name?" Alpheus asked.

"No."

He tightened his arm around her back and drew her more firmly against him. On the television in front of them, he'd switched to a nature documentary. A pack of wild dogs was closing in from all angles on a wildebeest.

"What is your real name?"

She answered, but he couldn't understand; she was crying heavily.

"A man once asked me why I like wild animals so much." *So, before I killed him, I told him.* "They don't pretend. They simply are." He pulled her tighter still so her forehead was now resting against his chin. "Do you think we pretend, Dolores?"

"No."

He lowered his lips so he could kiss her forehead. Then he opened his mouth and pressed his teeth against the same spot. He pressed in hard enough to cause her discomfort and to suggest he could bite if he so wished.

She whimpered and pleaded.

He drew back his head, ending his threat, and said, "We pretend. All of us. Don't you agree?"

"Yes ... of course ... yes."

He watched a wild dog chewing on the stomach of the great African antelope. "But wild animals don't. None of them. Think of the hawk, perched upon the tree branch next to the wetland. It waits for long periods of time. You think it's resting. But it isn't. Neither is it just pretending, like our deceitful species. It is just itself. Watching and waiting, and only when it feels there is gain to be had, it swoops."

She continued to sob against him.

"I am not pretending now, Dolores. I came to your apartment this afternoon because you took something very dear from me. At this moment, you can think of me as that proud hawk at the top of the wood, watching proudly over his dominion, like a god. With that pendant returned to me, I will have no need to swoop, as there is no gain to be had. Do you understand?"

"Yes."

"Good. Now, look up at me, tell me where my most precious possession is, and I will keep things how they are. I will keep you exactly how you are."

When Peter Sheenan opened his door, the last thing Jake expected was a puppy jumping at him. He knelt and stroked its golden head. "A lab retriever?"

"Name's Mason."

Jake stared up at his old friend from his crouching position. "Bloody hell, Peter."

"What?"

"Well, where do I start?"

Peter had been with the K9 corps in Vietnam. Thousands of lives had been owed to the dogs of Vietnam who, with handlers such as Peter Sheenan, had managed to sniff out a well-concealed enemy on countless occasions. The dog handlers had grown close to the animals. Peter owed his life to Prince, the dog he had handled. Following the close of the war, many of these poor dogs had been deemed surplus and had never returned home, including Prince. To soldiers such as Peter, this had been one of the war's worst atrocities.

"You said you could never have another dog after what you experienced. And wasn't Prince a lab too?"

"He was. And yes, you're right; I did say that. But times change. I've changed. I'm not getting any younger, and I'm craving some companionship in my twilight years."

"I'm not enough for you?"

"You're too much for me most of the time. That's part of the problem. Besides, I stupidly went to an animal shelter. I couldn't walk away from him after I'd seen him."

Jake stood up with Mason in his arms. The lab licked his face. "Easy, boy."

"I'll save you asking your next question. Mason was one of my best friends, so that's why he's got his name."

"Mason was bad, Peter."

"He was my friend."

"The things he did ..."

"The things *he* did, or the things *Liam* did?"

"I'm not getting into the semantics with you. People died violently at his hand, even if it was diminished responsibility. Do we really need reminding of it every time you say your new puppy's name?"

"Let's not get into it, then." Peter reached to take his

new friend. "The name is a testament to the goodness that existed in Mason Rogers—a goodness I cherished, and now miss. I will celebrate it if I so wish."

Jake held up his hands. "Whatever. I've been in Blue Falls long enough to know arguing with a stubborn, old local is doomed to failure."

"Stubborn, old local *Abernaki* Indian with more lives than a cat."

"Well, I guess that does give it more flavor. Anyway, nice to meet your new dog, but we need to hit the road. My phone has been rattling constantly in my pocket; there's only so long I can ignore Louise Price."

Peter pushed Mason into the house. "You go and piss and shit in there for a couple of hours." He closed and locked the door. "You could always just change your mind, tell this lieutenant what you know, and I can go back to housetraining a dog that is about to ruin my carpets."

Jake shook his head. "She sent me to the Holbrooks to not rattle them and get the truth. I got the truth." He shrugged. "Although I can't claim to have left them unrattled. Still, the same principle applies with Molly Holbrook. If she knows where Gabriel is, I don't want her rattled by the police. And I've got a secret weapon, the local sage."

Peter made a show of looking around. "Where is he, then?"

"People trust you, Peter. You calm them."

"I never manage to calm you."

"I'm different."

"Unhinged, definitely."

"Get in the fucking car, old man."

They had to come some way off the beaten track to get to Molly Holbrook's home. If the purpose of the journey hadn't been born from concern over Molly's links to a rampaging murderous paedophile, then it could have been considered a particularly pleasant one. The trees and fields were in full color, and overhead, a flock of birds had taken to a V-formation.

While Jake handled the driving, Peter pointed up at the birds. "Look! The winds are changing, and those birds are taking full advantage. Did you know that each set of wings creates a different current? They can then use the surrounding air in efficient ways to travel greater distances without rest."

"You sound like a nature documentary."

"Or I sound like a man who appreciates our insignificance. We had to design an airplane to be that aerodynamic."

"Pretty impressive that we did."

"Pretty impressive they didn't have to."

Jake parked.

As they walked across Molly's property, Peter said, "She certainly wanted out of civilization."

In his head, Jake imagined Gabriel's face folding in pleasure as he satisfied himself in one corner of a room while a young girl with red pig tails cried in another. "I don't think civilization was being all that good to her."

As they passed two other cars—neither of which Jake recognized as Gabriel's—they approached the front door. They heard the dogs barking around the enclosure at the side. "Well, if the twisted bastard is here, he *must* have got a warm reception!" Peter said.

As they ascended the steps to the porch, Jake nodded at

the rifle slung over Peter's back. "Just be careful with that. We are trying to be subtle."

"You want me to put it back in the car?"

"No. Maybe just wait at the bottom of the steps."

Peter nodded and headed down the steps.

Jake rang the doorbell.

Nothing.

He tried again before attempting a forceful knock, which also yielded nothing. He shuffled along to try to see inside the house, but the net curtains were very effective at keeping out wandering eyes. Jake turned. "Remind me of the nickname the redneck locals gave you again?"

"Dogman?"

"That's the one. Just remind me why you got it again?"

"You already know. K9 corps."

"No chance it was to do with your secret ability to communicate with dogs you've yet to tell me about?"

"No chance. Why?"

"Because we are about to go around the side of the house to the back, and I'm worried some of your furry friends might have something to say about that."

———

Peter's furry friends *did* have something to say about their presence, but fortunately, it was all said from behind bars. In fact, the only thing that impeded their progress to the back of the house was Peter himself, who felt compelled to stop to identify the different breeds of dogs.

Jake pulled his friend close so he could talk directly into his ear and be heard over his incessant barking. "Not the time."

Peter nodded.

Jake caught the snarl of a large Doberman from the corner of his eye. Froth dripped from its jagged teeth.

Months before, Peter had ventured to the MacLeoid property to free fighting dogs from their enclosure. Jake shuddered when he considered Peter's reckless approach that fated evening. "I had a large bag of treats with me."

"Were you ever worried they might consider you the treat?"

"Never crossed my mind. Guess we'll never know, anyhow. I got my teeth smashed to pieces by a psychotic farmer before I got to them."

Jake tried knocking on the back door, and when there was no answer, he said, "We're going in."

"I was worried you were going to say that."

Jake tried the handle. The door was unlocked. They entered through the kitchen. Jake held up a finger to Peter to instruct him to remain silent while he listened for sounds in the house. A pointless exercise—he could hear little over the barking dogs at the side of the house.

They crossed the kitchen. Jake noticed the pile of dirty crockery and a couple of sealed bin liners lying on their side by the trashcan. If this was someone living alone, they hadn't tended to basic cleaning tasks in a while. More likely, the waste had built up quickly due to people staying here.

"Are you ready with that?" Jake whispered, pointing at the rifle bouncing off Peter's chest.

"You've changed your tune."

"Something's definitely not right."

"Yes. I feel it too. Maybe we should just leave and contact the lieutenant."

Jake nodded. He turned and looked at the open back door, then that image of Gabriel, sweating and masturbating as his young victim watched, infiltrated his head again. He turned back. "No. We go on. He's dangerous, and if he's here, he could be up to his old tricks."

An inch at a time, Jake opened the kitchen door. He winced. He'd smelled death and decay at a crime scene before, but this was different somehow. It was tinged with the medicinal, like the pungent antiseptic smell found in hospitals.

He looked at Peter, who already had a hand to his mouth. Jake fully opened the door, checked once that Peter had his back with the raised rifle, and entered the hallway. He pinned himself to the wall and slid alongside it to the doorway. The rancid smell of death intensified, and he was forced to press one hand over his nose. The breaths that now went in through his mouth were cloying and only slightly more bearable.

Peter was now at the other side of the hallway, angling his rifle at the doorway Jake was flirting with.

"Is anyone here?" Jake asked and waited for a response, but he heard nothing over the disturbed canines outside. "We are armed," Jake said, louder now. "If anything happens when I turn into this room, my colleague will open fire."

The barking continued.

Jake sighed and nodded at Peter. He peered around the doorframe. He saw a smashed television, a coffee table piled with bloody rags, an open antiseptic bottle on the floor, a large white duvet, and—he felt the burn of acid in his stomach—two pairs of feet poking from beneath it. When he noticed the fiery-red hair from one of the two victims spilling out from beneath the top of the duvet, he thought back to the picture on Ethan Holbrook's wall and steadied himself against the doorframe.

FOUR DAYS BEFORE JAKE PETTMAN LEAVES BLUE FALLS

GRITTING HIS TEETH, Gabriel sanitized the knife wound on his arm, then inspected it. The butterfly strips were managing to hold the opening closed, and the flesh around it didn't look any angrier than it had the previous day, so he was fairly certain it was not infected—at least not yet.

With watering eyes, he slipped his collared shirt back on and fastened the buttons. *Fuck, Molly! Why did you have to go and spear me like that?*

He leaned forward on the sofa with his hands on his knees, taking long, deep breaths while waiting for the antiseptic liquid to stop clawing the germs from his wound. Once the agony subsided, he reached for a glass of water and some medication on the coffee table. He chased down two Tylenol with some Adderall—only *three*. Supply was running desperately low.

He stood and headed to the window overlooking Molly's porch and, beyond that, her driveway. Her cellphone was on the windowsill. He could see she'd had one mail message—a reply from the email he'd sent the previous day. He opened it. A cellphone number. Nothing else.

He called it, and while the phone rang, he wished out loud that the dogs would stop fucking yapping. But they didn't. They never did. Add to that the fact they were probably hungry. He was indifferent to dogs but didn't like to hear them suffer. However, going near those vicious fuckers wasn't an option.

"Yes." It was the same gruff male voice from the day before.

"I called. Then I emailed the address you gave me. Now I've called again. Are there any more hoops?"

"Tomorrow. Text me your location within five minutes. Any longer and this phone will already have been destroyed."

"I'll do it. Then can I relax? Or do I need to write and mail a letter to you for final confirmation?"

"Just remember, we see the money first, or it's a no-go." The phone went dead.

"No time to chat?" Gabriel asked. He texted the location and slid the cellphone into his pocket.

The sun was blazing outside. It was tempting to go for a stroll. A warm breeze may just distract him from the infernal burning in his left arm. But, of course, that was lunacy. *You're a fugitive now.*

He recalled the day he told his father, Earl, that he wanted to be a police officer. He remembered the pride on his daddy's face.

It's remarkable how far you've fallen, son.

I'm sorry, Dad. I tried. For so long, I tried, but these bastards inside me, these demons, well, I guess they just won out in the end.

Time passed at that windowsill. Then came the hit of amphetamine. His eyes widened. The chewing of gum began. The gash in his arm throbbed a cadence with his now-heavy heartbeat; however, with the drug in his system, he definitely gave less of a fuck about the injury. He was ready to move on. Put all this behind him. Start a new life ...

He heard a car come into Molly's driveway.

Gabriel moved quickly, accidently knocking over the open bottle of antiseptic on the coffee table. "Shit." The pungent odor leapt into the air.

He hurdled the blood-splattered duvet and raced through the open lounge door. In the hallway, he briefly considered sprinting upstairs for the rifle, but then he noticed the locked front door and decided to remain positive that it wouldn't come to that. He darted down the hallway and peered through the peephole.

A lanky man, who was still to be informed that mullets really weren't fashionable anymore, climbed the porch steps. At least he'd not opted for the handlebar moustache. He wore a long-sleeved gray shirt and skin-tight black jeans. Had the man not noticed the incredible heat before getting dressed? Gabriel wasn't surprised to see sweat patches blooming from under his arms.

As the man neared, Gabriel was glad the dogs had upped their volume further; there was no chance of this visitor hearing his breathing from behind the door.

The man rapped his knuckles on the door, waited, then stepped backward, looking frustrated. "Molly?" He came in for the second knock.

Gabriel felt the wood that his face was touching vibrate.

The man tried a *third* time. "Molly? It's Logan!"

Okay, Logan, you streak of piss, now is the time for you to fuck off, for your own good.

Through the peephole, Gabriel watched Logan take a few steps backward and eye the door suspiciously. Eventually, he turned and walked away.

"Good boy."

Gabriel returned to the lounge, winced over the intense medicinal smell, slammed the door behind him, and flopped onto the sofa. Tomorrow morning suddenly seemed so long away. The Adderall had him wired, but he closed his eyes, nevertheless. After the last few days of sensory overload, a sensory shutdown would be very welcome.

Outside, the dogs continued with their cacophony. *Fucking bitches.*

Again, he saw his father's proud face. *I promise to make amends, Daddy. I promise to make everything good again. I'll find somewhere new—*

"Molly?"

Gabriel's eyes bolted open. He sucked in a sharp breath and jumped to his feet.

"Molly, are you in?"

The fucker, Logan, was in the house.

Cursing himself for leaving the back door unlocked, Gabriel dove for the blood-stained duvet on the floor. He tore it off Molly's prone body and reached for the hilt of the knife buried deep in the back of her head. It didn't come loose on the first pull. Fuck! He'd jammed it in hard.

"Molly, I'm getting worried now."

Shit, Logan was almost at the lounge door!

He knelt on her back, put both hands on the hilt, and yanked. He thought of Arthur pulling Excalibur from the stone. The knife slipped free at the same time the handle on the lounge door came down. *Thump – thump.*

What was that?

The handle flipped back up. Logan must have released it. *Thump – thump.*

Upstairs! Stamping. The floor was shaking.

"Molly, are you all right up there?" Logan shouted.

Bloody knife now in hand, Gabriel went through the lounge door. He looked up to see Logan's boots at the top of the stairs, then disappear onto the landing.

Thump – Thump.

He would be too late in stopping Logan making his discovery, but he wouldn't be too late in *stopping* Logan. Coming through the back door was the worst, and last, mistake that lanky, mullet-wearing fool would ever make. He quietly climbed the stairs. When Gabriel turned from the final step, he saw Logan at the end of the landing opening the farthest door. Gabriel started down the landing, keeping his footfall light.

"Oh shit," Logan said after opening the door. "Are you okay?"

Gabriel listened to the muffled response which made no sense and closed the gap between him and the intruder.

"I'll get you out—"

Gabriel looped his arm around the thin man's neck. Then, from behind Logan, he stared into Kayla's wide and desperate eyes.

She gave a muffled cry through the gag he'd wedged into her mouth. Her left arm was against her chest in a rudimentary sling he'd fashioned the previous night after winging her with his rifle. It was bloodstained and already in dire need of a change. Her other hand was handcuffed to the bedrest. However, despite the uncomfortable position he'd been forced to leave her in, the clever girl had managed to kick over the bedside table and, subsequently, had reached it with her foot to stamp on its side.

Gabriel dragged Logan free of the door. "I won't make you watch this again, Kayla," he said and kicked the door shut with his left foot.

He dragged Logan, who fought uselessly against his right arm, partway down the landing before cutting his throat with the same knife he'd used to kill his girlfriend.

6

THE DAY BEFORE JAKE PETTMAN LEAVES
BLUE FALLS

"DOES HE HAVE no limits?" Jake kicked the stone wall that enclosed the driveway. "Torturing her as an innocent girl, and then killing her as an innocent woman?"

"I'm sorry, Jake." From behind, Peter's hand closed on his shoulder.

"It's not me who needs your sympathy. It's *that* poor family. Willow, Ethan ... they've just lost everything."

"Don't forget, you were related to her, Jake."

Jake spun, freeing himself from Peter's consoling grip, and pointed at him. "We're not *fucking* going there, old man." Jake looked down. "Besides, nothing changes. We need to find them."

"And then what?"

Jake looked up at him. "Let's just find them first, okay?

Cross that bridge when we come to it." Jake reached into his pocket and thumbed the piece of paper he'd found by the bloody rags on the coffee table. He shouldn't have picked it up, really, but the words written on it had compelled him. He'd already promised himself he would hand it to Louise as soon as she arrived.

Speak of the devil ...

Headed by Louise's Audi, the driveway filled quickly. Most of the cars belonged to officers from the Blue Falls PD, but the occasional Audi indicated that Louise had enlisted further support from the Maine State Police.

The dogs around the side didn't like it.

"I'm going to feed them," Peter said.

"Are you insane?"

"Didn't you see them? I doubt they've been fed in a week."

"That's my point. What do you think they'll see when you open the cage doors? A kind man or sustenance?"

"Only one way to find out. There's an enclosure in front of them. I'll see if there's some kibble or something in there." Peter disappeared around the side of the house.

Jake noticed Lillian among a small group of officers heading onto the porch.

She met his eyes.

He waved a greeting to her, but didn't get one in return.

The officers went through the front door that he had unlocked for them from the inside.

Louise didn't follow the officers onto the porch; instead, she marched straight toward him.

He knew she was pissed, but how pissed was still to be determined, because she *always* walked ramrod straight and looked down the length of her nose at those she talked to. She struggled as she drew nearer as Jake was considerably taller than her. "Lost your cellphone, Mr. Pettman?"

"I phoned you, didn't I?"

"Yes, after missing the ten or so calls I made to you."

Jake sighed. "Sorry. I was a policeman. *Once*. When you get the scent, you get the scent, I guess."

"I'm all for instincts, but common sense is what keeps people alive."

"True, but I'm trumped by a little girl out there desperate to stay alive."

"How do you know I wasn't referring to her?"

Jake sighed again.

"I'm making the point that gallivanting off like a cowboy will only put more people in danger."

"You've made your point."

Louise nodded, narrowing her eyes.

Jake gripped the paper in his pocket. Louise would initially tear him to pieces for tampering with a crime scene, but after she'd thought about it, she may come to accept his instinctual behavior. After all, it was a result of his background as a detective. She may start to appreciate him as a resource and keep him on the same page in the investigation. He hoped so. He desperately wanted to see this through.

"I've only got myself to blame," Louise said.

Jake lifted out the paper. "It's not your fault. I thought, rightly or wrongly, Molly's link to the Bickfords may make her more receptive to me—in the same way, we thought that about her parents."

"I shouldn't have called you in. I got desperate. This is over." Louise started to turn.

"Hang on a minute, Lieutenant—"

She turned back. "*No,* you hang on. You're predictable.

73

Very predictable. I knew that before but stupidly gave you a chance. You're done." She turned toward the house. "Now, if you'll excuse me, I have to go and secure the crime scene."

"I'm *not* done."

Marching away, Louise said, "You've been done for a long time, Jake Pettman."

"Fuck you," Jake mumbled, slamming the paper back into his pocket. *I'm done when I say I'm done.*

Alpheus's trip to the taxi depot had been short. Small mercies. The place was rank with the odor of exploitation. The hawk was a free bird. Alpheus was a free man. He cherished everything this meant.

Upstairs, above the taxi depot, escorts gathered in tiny rooms. The man left in charge of them was large and skilled at hurting, but not as skilled as Alpheus. However, just as he hadn't needed to kill Dolores, he didn't need to kill the large man.

Just the fact that he was there, that he was watching, that he *could* swoop—that was enough.

In Dolores's case, he'd simply told her this. Unfortunately, in the large man's case—at least, for him—he had to be *shown.* One plucked eyeball later, chewed like a sweetmeat, all was well, and the large man had given him Tucker Cobb's address.

Tucker had left his front door unlocked. To do that in this day and age? *What a peculiar man.*

At the foot of the peculiar man's stairs, holding his weapon of choice—a Para-Ordnance P18—Alpheus stopped and listened.

Silence. Alpheus was confident that he was alone on

Tucker's ground floor. Then he locked onto a conversation. He heard a deep, male voice, potentially Tucker's. He couldn't hear the other voice in the conversation, indicating he may be on a phone call.

Alpheus ascended the stairs and tracked the sound of the lopsided conversation all the way to the third door. At this closer distance, he could recognize Tucker's voice, having spoken to him by phone when negotiating visits from his escorts. There was still no other voice, leading Alpheus to the conclusion that he must, indeed, be on the phone.

Alpheus opened the door and saw his unwitting host hunched over an elderly, bedridden woman. He aimed his P18.

"Who are you?" Tucker asked.

"You are not what I imagined," Alpheus said.

"That voice. I recognize it. You made a mess of some of my girls."

"Were you not warned? Were you not paid well?"

The pimp looked away. He was a squat, overweight man with thinning, dishevelled hair. His gray clothing fit him badly. "How did you find me?"

"I went to the depot. I spoke to the man you left in charge. He *saw* what I was. Interestingly, I will be the last thing he sees clearly."

"You killed him?"

"No. He's alive. I've just altered him. It was you I came to kill."

Tucker released the woman's wrinkled hand and started to stand.

"Stay seated," Alpheus said, slightly lifting the silenced P18.

"You can't kill me in front of my mother! There are lines! Surely, there are lines?"

His mother murmured something. It made no sense. It only indicated that she was alive.

"You took from me."

"I don't know what you're talking about."

Alpheus came down the other side of the bed. He held the weapon with his favored left hand, so he let the fingertips of his right hand trace the edge of the duvet. Eventually, his fingers settled on Tucker's mother's hand.

"Please leave her alone."

Alpheus looked down at her face.

"How old is she?"

"Ninety-four."

Her eyes were tiny and buried deep in loose, wrinkled skin, but they still flickered with life, albeit with little awareness.

"She doesn't fully understand the world anymore."

"She hasn't for a long time," Tucker said.

"Cruel."

"Age is cruel."

"Not age, Tucker. *You*. It is you who is cruel."

"I don't understand."

Keeping the gun trained on Tucker, Alpheus stroked the old woman's face. "I thrive on awareness. I revel in clarity and the ability to focus. Without these things, what are we really?"

"Why are you here? What is it you think I have done?"

Alpheus lifted his hand from Tucker's mother's face and held a finger in the air. "Hush, Tucker. Hush. We will get there. Cruelty carries heavy punishments, but I may give you a chance to atone."

Tucker put his hands to his head. "I don't understand."

"When my mother lost everything I hold dear—awareness, clarity, focus—I turned off the empty vessel. Looking at your mother now, I wonder, how you could not have done the same?"

"It's my mother. My *mother*! I love her. How could I do what you're suggesting?"

"It's actually quite easy. Your mother has gone. Know that and know that killing her is a courtesy. When I put that pillow over my mother's head, I knew she was gone, but I have so much left, so much of her in here"—he tapped his head—"and"—he touched his heart—"in here. *So much*. You took something from me Tucker Cobb. Something of great value."

"I don't know. I really don't know."

"Hush again." Alpheus took a deep breath. "Either you or Dolores lies. What I saw in Dolores's eyes when I told her how close she was to her end suggests to me that it wasn't her. Listen, Tucker, I see a familiar chain around your mother's neck."

"This doesn't make any sense—"

"It looks so much like the one I have held in my hands *so* many times."

Tucker gulped and shook his head. "I-I ..."

"Undo the top button of your mother's blouse. Show me what hangs at the end of that chain."

"I can't! Please! I really don't know—"

"Show me, or I will tear off her head. I will tear off her head and let that chain fall from her torn neck."

Tucker started to cry.

"Show me!"

Tucker undid the top buttons of his mother's blouse and looked up at Alpheus. His face was blemished. His piggy eyes were red, and his fat lips quivered.

"That is identical to my mother's pendant."

"I'm sorry ... so sorry ..."

"Now, *Tucker,* open the pendant."

Tucker shook his head. "No, I-I can't."

Alpheus peeled off one of his gloves and spread his palm in the air, exposing his sharpened nails. "Do you see my fingers?"

Tucker nodded, snot running down his face.

"I can tear, Tucker. I can tear ever so well."

Tucker reached forward and opened the pendant. He slipped back into his chair with his hands over his mouth.

"Who is that in my mother's pendant?"

Tucker's voice was muffled both by his hands and his tears, but Alpheus understood. "That's me and ... and her."

"How sweet, Tucker. Where is the original picture?"

Tucker shook his head. "I'm sorry. I had no idea. Dolores told me she got it from a customer, but she never said it was you. If she'd told me it was you, I never would have taken it. If she'd told me—goddamn her—if she'd told me, I would have returned it."

"Where is the picture, Tucker?"

"Fuck, fuck, fuck—"

"Where?"

"I threw it away. I'm sorry. It might still be in the—"

"Hush." Alpheus straightened his back and listened to it crack. He tilted his head back, looked up the ceiling, and took a long, deep breath. He levelled his gaze at Tucker and flicked his head from one shoulder to the other, causing another loud crack. "I'm going to give you a choice."

"A choice?"

"Yes, one that allows you to live. Would you like that?"

"Yes! Yes, please!"

"The choice. Either I kill you or I take from you what you took from me. How does that sound?"

"Perfect. Of course, take it! Take it back!" Tucker leaned over to undo the pendant around his mother's neck.

"No, Tucker, not the pendant. The pendant is useless without the picture, and it seems you have destroyed that. So, *worm*, I ask you again. I can kill you or take from you what you took from me?"

"What does that mean? I don't know what that means!"

"Sit back, and I'll show you. I'll just need a nod."

Tucker sat back in the chair. His fat face glistened with sweat. His head moving up and down look more like an out-of-control muscle spasm than a frenetic nod.

"Good." Alpheus reached into the pocket of his dirty, gray leather jacket. "If you move, Tucker, I will shoot. Do you understand?"

Another nod.

Alpheus pulled a purple plastic box from his pocket. He still had the P18 trained on Tucker, but he managed to pop it open one-handedly. He laid the open box on the bed beside Tucker's mother and plucked out his veneer.

"What is that?" Tucker asked, a tremble in his voice.

"A hawk possesses a hooked beak for biting and tearing flesh. Our own teeth are too blunt to make that effective. I had this made especially." He clipped the resin veneer to his top row of teeth. He pulled in his bottom lip so the stainless-steel hook, which aligned perfectly with his two front teeth, reached down a couple of inches but didn't scrape against his chin. Alpheus leaned toward Tucker's mother's face.

Tucker lurched forward. "No, stop. *No!*"

Alpheus pulled the trigger. There was a muffled *thwap*, and Tucker was sitting back in the chair again, dying and clutching a bloody hole in the center of his stomach.

"No, no, no ..." His voice faded, as did the color in his skin.

Alpheus didn't want to waste a single moment. He *so* wanted Tucker to see this before he vacated this earth. He laid his P18 on the bed next to the box which protected his veneer, slipped his hand beneath the elderly woman's head, and swooped for her face with his hooked beak bared.

7

J AKE WAITED UNTIL he was on Peter's sofa, with Mason sitting there licking his feet, before fessing up to taking the note from the crime scene.

"Come again?" Peter said.

"I found this." Jake pulled the note he'd found on Molly's coffee table and threw it onto Peter's.

"You just lifted evidence from that bloodbath?"

"It's complicated."

"Yes, it is. Also, it's just plain wrong."

"I know. I was going to hand it over."

"Why didn't you?"

"I lost my temper. She was being difficult."

"It's her job to be difficult."

Jake leaned forward. "Anyway, Peter, enough of this holier-than-thou bullshit. Your choices over the past few months haven't earned you a nomination for the Blue Falls Citizen of the Year Award either."

Mason sauntered to his master and whined to be picked up.

Peter obliged and nodded at the note. "What is it?"

"So, now you're interested?"

"Of course. No harm in knowing before we hand it back over to that lieutenant."

"Bit late for that."

"Jesus, Jake. What've you done?"

"It's an email address, so I emailed—"

"No, you didn't."

"Yes, I did. When I told you I was writing a message to Piper in the car."

"So, you lied to me?"

"Yes, in the same way that you said you were just going to feed Molly's dogs but were really smoking."

"I *did* feed the dogs. That was always my priority."

"So, you didn't smoke?"

"I didn't say that."

Jake smiled. "We all have secrets."

"These *two* secrets are not the same."

"True. Yours is definitely going to kill you."

"Precisely why I told you I quit! Life is easier with a few white lies. Anyway, enough of that bullshit. Did you email from your own account?"

"No. I set up one. Takes a minute."

"Hopefully not in my name! What did you write?"

"I simply wrote, *I was given this e-mail. I think you can help.*"

"Why?"

Jake shrugged. "It was all I could think of writing."

"Did it work?"

"I got a message back asking, *How?* It was rather enigmatically signed 'C'"

"And?"

"I wrote, *You know how.*"

Peter rolled his eyes. "Jesus, you and this unknown

recipient are a right pair of conversationalists!"

"Well, it worked. They sent me a cellphone number."

"They didn't!" Peter sat back in his chair, stroking Mason. "Shit, Jake, this really does sound like we need to get the lieutenant involved."

"I suggest we let it play out. We could spook whoever we just hooked."

"Are you sure this isn't some vigilante mission? You've had a hard-on for Gabriel ever since you walked into town."

Some time alone with Gabriel would be nice. "No, that's not it. I just want to find this girl—if you need a job done properly, and all that."

"Sounds like arrogance."

Jake dismissed his criticism with a shake of his head. "I remember you saying you kept spare cellphones when you worked on the Abenaki council way back when."

Peter nodded. "I gave out more than one. The situations some of my kind have found themselves in over the years!" He sighed. "Well, you know about Felicity, don't you? God rest her soul. With these phones, they knew they could contact me or anyone else without anyone finding out."

"Have you got any left?"

"You're going to call that number, aren't you?"

"I'm going to phone that number."

Peter sighed and stood. "Let me look." He handed his puppy to Jake. "But make sure you get to know Mason. I can't afford a dog walker, and these old legs aren't what they once were."

"Can we change his name then?"

"No."

Thirty minutes later, following the use of a charging lead, Jake was standing alone in Peter's kitchen with the door shut and a cellphone pinned to his ear which could double as a kid's plastic toy. *No expense spared here, Peter!*

"Yes?" a gravelly voice answered.

"Is this C?"

"Who wants to know?"

"J."

"Not enough."

"It'll have to be."

"Well, J, speak. This phone has a best-before date of two minutes. How can I help you?"

"I need your service."

"Which one?"

Jake sweated. *How the fuck would I know? I don't know what you do!* "The premium?"

The man's laugh was gravelly too. "Destination?"

Jake ran a hand over his cropped head. *A transport company? Drugs?* "Canadian border."

A lingering silence.

Jake kicked a bowl of dog food. *Have I blown it?* "Hello?"

"When?"

"Soon."

"That's not good enough."

Jake felt like he was on fire. He opened the fridge door for the cool air. "This will be the biggest deal you've ever seen."

"I doubt it. Product and quantity?"

Jake's mouth fell open. He was in the US, not the UK. He couldn't be sure of the slang terms, or even the method they used for quantities. "I'm not convinced of your credentials. I want to discuss in person, C."

"That's not an option."

"Then the deal goes elsewhere."

"Elsewhere it goes."

Jake slammed the fridge door. *Think, goddammit, think
...*

"We are approaching the best-before date, J. Is there anything else I can help you with?"

Jake took a deep breath. *The last throw of the dice.* "Truth be known, the exact numbers are astronomical. That conversation has to be a personal one."

"That's not how we do business."

"I worked with Jotham MacLeoid. That's how we did business."

"Jotham MacLeoid?"

There it was. For the first time, interest in that voice. Seize on it. "I have other calls to make, C. I have a lot of product. A lot. It's burning a hole in my sleeping time. I need to move it on. My best-before date is also almost up. I'm afraid—"

"Write this down. One hour. Don't be late, or I won't be there."

Jake wrote down the address. "See you there, C."

The phone was already dead.

Jake looked down at the address.

Bingo.

THREE DAYS BEFORE JAKE PETTMAN
LEAVES BLUE FALLS

GABRIEL LOOKED AT the high-roof Ford Transit.

"The girl?" the driver asked, eyeing Kayla.

85

"None of your business."

The driver adjusted the sleeves on his dirty overalls, which were worn to make him look more like a mechanic than a drug smuggler. He spat tobacco. "She's handcuffed to you."

"*Still* none of your business."

"And what happened to her arm?"

Kayla looked up. "He's a murderer—"

"*Shut up!*" Gabriel said, yanking the cuffs.

She squealed.

"Speak like that again before we're out of the state, and I'll put the gag back on." He removed a wad of cash from his jeans pocket and threw it to the driver. "From now on, our conversation revolves solely around this service. Do you understand?"

The driver nodded and spat more brown gunk onto the ground. He opened the transit van door. It was piled high with engines, wheels, exhausts, and other loose car parts.

"It's full of crap," Gabriel said. "Where are we supposed to go?"

The driver climbed into the transit, maneuvered around and over the side of a small pile of car doors, then pointed down in the center. "Out of sight, out of mind. The floor has been raised for a compartment beneath."

"Not enough by the looks of it!"

"Anymore and it would be noticeable. Because the van has a high roof, it remains less conspicuous. There's room for you two to lay flat underneath, but be aware, you may slide about. I'll try to drive as slow as I can. You may consider removing the handcuffs, especially with one of her arms in a sling. She needs to be able to brace herself against the side if necessary."

"If you are going to drive slow, then why would it be necessary?"

The driver chewed, shrugged, and smiled. "You think this is a low-risk gig?"

"I'm just thinking, get it right, young man, get it right."

"And I will, old man, just like I have done every time before. But take my advice on the handcuffs, and be aware that we are stopping by my garage first to put some more stuff in the back. The van must be completely full to make the false floor as inconspicuous as possible. You will be trapped in though. The trapdoor will be completely covered."

"No, no, I can't ..." Kayla said.

Gabriel looked at her. "It won't be long; I promise."

"I can't! I'm claustrophobic." Her face paled.

"I'll remove the handcuffs while we are under. I promise."

"It won't be enough."

"I'm sorry, Kayla, but it'll have to be."

"It won't be pleasant, girl." The driver smiled. "Almost like being buried alive."

Kayla gave a short gasp.

"That's not helping," Gabriel said.

"Sorry. It's the first time I've ever done this with people. I'm finding it very intriguing. Also, you can't have any light down their either in case they see it through the air holes, so keep those cells off."

"Have they ever searched your van when you've done this before?"

"They've flashed their torches around, of course, but have they ever hoisted oily car parts out the back before? No. So, you can take some comfort in that."

"Thanks, you've put us completely at ease."

"It's what it is. Take it or leave it."

"Let's go."

Gabriel had expected the fake compartment to be bad but not quite this bad. The lack of ventilation, combined with its proximity to the exhaust, quickly turned it into an oven.

A bottle of water would have been nice—or, at the very least, a warning to bring one.

The compartment was almost the same size as the floor of the transit, so it was difficult to stop the sliding when the vehicle was on the road. Gabriel found the best option was to remain wedged near the bottom corner.

As promised, he removed Kayla's handcuffs. Then he kept hold of her hand, because his bulkier frame kept him and, as a result, her steadier.

She didn't fight his grip. She was claustrophobic and terrified, whereas the only thing bothering him was the heat. His entire body was now drenched in sweat, and he was becoming increasingly concerned that the temperature could actually kill them. He thought he could smell exhaust fumes too, but he hoped this was just paranoia, because that could easily be game over.

At the driver's pitstop, Gabriel felt every vibration of the extra car parts as they landed on the false floor of the transit. Kayla panicked while the spare parts were completely closing off their route from the concealed compartment. She buried her head in his shoulder. Stroking her hair and comforting her suddenly felt like the most natural thing in the world to Gabriel, and he prayed that away from this situation, she would remember and appreciate a moment that, in any other life, could be considered paternal.

The driver kept his promise to drive slowly, but Gabriel soon wished he would move quicker. Grogginess was rearing its ugly head, and he didn't know how long he could hold on to consciousness.

"Are you all right?" he asked Kayla.

She responded with a sob, and he felt some relief.

The van stopped and remained stationary for quite some time.

Are we at the checkpoint? Gabriel fought to stay awake. He longed for an Adderall, but it would be too awkward to locate the bottle in the confined darkness.

The van inched forward, then paused for another while.

A queue. Yes, the checkpoint. "We must be quiet now, Kayla."

"I can't see much."

The airholes had allowed some light into the compartment. It had taken their eyes a short time to reach optimal sensitivity to low-light conditions, and when they had, the results had been very disappointing. Kayla was a blurred shadow to him, as he would be to her.

"Me neither," Gabriel said. "But I'm here, and I got you."

"I need to get out."

He stroked her damp forehead. "Soon, my dear. I promise, soon." He wanted to kiss her forehead and apologize for shooting her the day before last, but he held back; now was not the time.

His breath caught in his throat; the driver was in conversation with someone.

The engine died. Light flickered through the airholes alongside both sides of the compartment. Torches.

Their turn.

He drew Kayla tight against him when he heard the clunk of the transit door open. He imagined the torches sweeping over the vehicle parts. He put a finger to Kayla's mouth, instructing her not to say anything. He left his hand hovering there, ready to slam it over her mouth if necessary.

"Surprised the van moves! You sure you're not over on weight?" an officer asked.

"Not a pound over," the driver said.

"If your brakes fail, this thing will be like a cannonball!"

"Which is why I get it serviced twice a year. It's all in the documentation I gave your colleague."

"My old man used to break cars," the officer said. "I don't remember him driving all over with what he foraged though."

"These are specialist pieces. Mainly old Porsche and other sporty makes. Wouldn't trust any of our transit companies with this gear! Plus, they charge an arm and a leg to shift engines and such."

"Fair enough. Looks like you've got yourself a nice earner here. I'm going to have to look around."

"That's fine. I knew the roads were being monitored, that's why I wore my overalls. One time, when I crossed the Canadian border, I was wearing some brand-new white Nike sneakers and my favorite Levi's. You can be sure I won't ever make that mistake again. If I start with the engines, could you give me a hand? Two-man job them."

"I can't breathe in here," Kayla said.

Gabriel put his finger to her mouth again.

"Let me breathe. Please."

He leaned in and whispered, "Kayla, you need to be quiet, or I will have to put my hand over your mouth."

She seemed to heed the warning.

Gabriel heard the thump of the driver's boots on the false floor above them and the heavy scratching sound as someone dragged an engine. He felt Kayla's hot breath against his finger.

"You ready, Officer?" the driver asked.

Gabriel expected to hear the footfalls of the officer as he climbed into the back of the transit. He drew in his finger and opened his large hand, preparing to smother Kayla's mouth if the terrified girl succumbed to temptation.

"Something's bothering me," the officer said.

Gabriel's heart rate accelerated.

"What's that, Officer?" the driver asked.

The sweat running from Gabriel's brow would surely be dripping onto Kayla's face.

"My back," the officer said, with a laugh. "It's fine. I've had a good look over. No need to empty it all out."

"You sure?"

"Positive! If you're hiding anything in there, you won't be getting it uphill anyway!" He laughed again.

The driver laughed too. "Well, I appreciate it. Got a long drive, and lugging that in and out would have been exhausting. Appreciate it."

The back of the van slammed shut. Gabriel sighed. If the carbon monoxide or the heat didn't get him, he would drown in a puddle of anxiety-induced sweat.

"Good girl. Just a moment longer," he said to Kayla and kissed her forehead.

She recoiled, but he tried not to let it bother him. *They were through. Freedom beckoned.*

When everything calmed down, that would be the time

to heal, that would be the time she would come to accept him.

The engine flared back to life, and the transit moved away.

The driver had suggested that being in this compartment would be like being buried alive. He hadn't been far wrong, but the joy and relief flowing through Gabriel's veins right now were a match for it. If it didn't have the potential to turn into the costliest mistake he'd ever made, he would have whooped with delight.

Beside him, Kayla wept.

"I will make it up to you, Kayla. I will make it *all* up to you."

The van accelerated, and Gabriel stretched himself out in the corner again to keep that stability; he gripped Kayla's hand as he had done before.

They'd only been driving another minute or so when the van halted again.

Gabriel knew this neck of the woods. There was no stop light less than a minute from that checkpoint. In fact, there was no stoplight anywhere near it—just open road. The driver should be speeding toward freedom.

What's going on? He heard the *thunk* of a car door slamming behind them. *Shit! The idiot has been pulled over!* Gabriel saw the torchlight again flickering through the airholes. *Shit ... shit ...*

He hadn't heard the van door open yet, so he assumed the driver was still behind the wheel. He imagined he'd be lowering his window about now.

"Officer? Everything okay?" the driver asked.

"Could you step out, sir? I just want to show you something."

Gabriel's heart beat quickly again as he heard the *thunk* of the door opening.

"Changed your mind on getting your hands dirty?" the driver asked, laughing, trying to make jovial a suddenly deteriorating situation.

"This way please," the officer said.

Leaving the engine running, the driver slammed the door behind him to follow.

The voices grew muffled as they moved from the open window at the front of the transit. Gabriel strained to hear the conversation at the rear of the transit. He made out very little, but when he heard the word, "Taillight," he felt hope spring inside him. When the driver and the officer reached the front of the vehicle and clarity returned to the conversation, Gabriel again felt that incredible sense of relief.

"I'll get that fixed at the next station along, Officer," the driver said.

"See that you do. Have a good evening, sir."

Despite the discomfort, Gabriel managed a smile. *What a fucking rollercoaster this was!*

Then Kayla, who he'd neglected to keep an eye on during this unanticipated moment, screamed at the top of her lungs.

8

THE DAY BEFORE JAKE PETTMAN LEAVES
BLUE FALLS

"EVER FEEL LIKE you're all on your own, Officer Sanborn?" Louise asked, pacing behind her desk.

"Most days, Lieutenant," Lillian said.

She pointed at the window that looked over the department floor. "Roll up those blinds and take a look at your colleagues."

"Why, ma'am?"

"To behold the cave of ignorance you work in."

"I don't need to. I already know what they're like."

"Of course, you do." Louise sighed. "You've had to suffer them a lot longer than I have."

"I know you don't want to hear this, ma'am, but that's why, you know, I listened to Jake Pettman."

"You're right; I don't want to hear it."

"I'm just saying he's not like those out there, ma'am. He really does care."

"I know he cares, Officer Sanborn. Too much. That's the problem. He's a loose cannon."

"I agree, but he's also, I don't know, instinctive? I don't think I've ever met anyone quite like him. If we let him help, we may get to the chief quicker. More importantly, we may get to Kayla quicker."

Louise shook her head. "No, Officer. Once was enough. I trusted him, and he let me down. He chose not to act within my parameters." She put her hand on the desk next to the framed photograph of her missing family. "His association with this case is done. Are we clear on that, Officer Sanborn?"

Lillian nodded. She lowered her head to try to hide her frustration.

"You sure ... *Lillian*?"

Lillian looked up. She couldn't remember the last time Louise had addressed her by her first name. "Yes, ma'am."

"Good. I trust you, like I trusted you with the situation involving Mason Rogers. Now that Ewan has gone, you're one of the few people left I can trust."

Lillian flinched at the mention of Ewan—a man she'd developed feelings for, a man who Gabriel had felled before those feelings could be realized.

Louise took a phone call. She nodded a few times, then gave a few instructions. Afterward, she told Lillian the outcome of the call. "They just found Ewan's Audi, the one Gabriel apprehended, in a patch of woods near Molly Holbrook's house. I've just shifted some CSI over there from the house. I'm sure they'll welcome the break from the smell."

Lillian felt a wave of nausea. She'd been one of the first

officers to see Molly and Logan. Her chief, a man she'd once admired, had made a right mess of that young, innocent couple.

"Both Molly's and Logan's vehicles were present at the scene. It's possible that Gabriel and Kayla left on foot. I've dispatched the dogs to see if they can trace a scent. It doesn't help that Molly's house was in the middle of nowhere. I've sent officers to the nearest homes, but they are some distance away, so it's a longshot. But you never know; they may have seen some comings and goings. Obviously, I've told the officers to try to get a look in those homes, in case they are hiding in there." She pulled her hand back and knocked over the picture of her three daughters. As Louise righted it, her gaze lingered on it for a moment, and Lillian saw overwhelming pain in that expression—the kind of pain only experienced by the most unfortunate of people in this world. "I'll let you know if I need you, Officer Sanborn."

Lillian stood. "Sorry if I speak out of turn, ma'am, but I'm just curious. Why did you choose to stay?"

Louise shrugged. "It's my job."

"Didn't the job finish?"

They had, indeed, solved the mystery surrounding the girl who had washed up on the banks of the Skweda.

"I offered my services in helping locate Kayla and Gabriel. As I was already here, those above, God bless them, thought it was appropriate that I stayed."

Lillian noticed a twitch in the corner of Louise's mouth. "I guess that makes sense, ma'am."

"Yes." Louise's face seemed to be paler now, and she was still gripping the photograph.

Lillian turned to exit.

"No, actually, wait."

Lillian turned back.

"I'm lying to you. You deserve better than that." She took a deep breath. "Listen, this is not the first time I've been to Blue Falls."

Lillian tried to hide the confusion from her expression and simply nodded. "I don't remember seeing you before."

"Because I kept a low profile. It wasn't work related."

"You've friends or family here?"

"No. Sit back down. Please, Lillian."

There it was again, her first name.

Louise circled the room and, using a key, locked the office door. She brushed the lowered blinds on the way to her desk, reassuring herself that no wayward eyes would find their way into the room. She went behind the desk, opened her top drawer, and looked at Lillian again before removing anything. "Coming to Blue Falls for work means I don't have to keep a low profile." She pulled out a thick brown folder.

"I don't understand."

"Don't play ignorant, Lillian. Ewan told you. I saw it in your eyes the day you walked in here with him after you staked out the Rogers general store."

Lillian's blood ran cold. "He … He … mentioned you'd—"

"Open it." She slid the folder across the desk.

Lillian obliged. Sitting on top of a mountain of documents was a postcard of a large rock which jutted a foot from a river. Water, which had clearly been airbrushed, splashed high up the rock and cascaded down the other side. In the bottom left corner was written, *Blue Falls.* Lillian turned it over and read the back.

Lou, this is the place I told you about. Blue Falls! I stopped in overnight again. Obviously not on this rock (although it might have been better than the motel I ended up in). Shame I must head north to sort through more incompetence early tomorrow! Don't worry, Florida not in doubt, but I might pencil in this place for a short summer break. Love you, Robert x

She looked up.

Louise was leaning forward on the table, staring at her.

"Your husband visited here."

"Many times. He worked as a business analyst and worked closely with a company based not far north of here. That postcard came during his first visit. Over the next couple of years, he visited Blue Falls many times en route to that company. I think he kind of appreciated the smalltown charm. After years of him visiting, he stopped mentioning it. I assumed it had grown samey."

"Did he disappear from here?"

"I'm not sure. The log at the New Lincoln Hotel indicates he checked in and out six years ago. He never made it to the company for his meeting though. He completely dropped off the radar. Then, two days later, my three children also disappeared. Coincidence?"

Lillian felt a tightening in her chest. This land was highly charged with loss and deep emotions; should she currently be going there?

"Well, knowing what I know about Blue Falls now, compared to what I knew then, I'd be more inclined to opt for it not being a coincidence." Louise spoke quicker now, and her eyes were wider.

Lillian responded in the safest way she knew how: a simple nod.

"By all means, Lillian, look through that folder. It's burned into my memory anyhow. I hope you get further than me." Her head dropped. "I'm at a loss."

Lillian opened her mouth to respond, but nothing came out. She had no idea what to say.

Louise's head remained low for some time, and she looked lost in thought.

Sadness of this magnitude was something Lillian had no experience with. When the silence became unbearable, she finally managed to say, "Of course, if that's what—"

The phone rang.

Louise lifted her head. Her sad eyes narrowed and sharpened again. She picked up the phone. "Lieutenant Louise Price. Can I help you?" She listened. "Finally! I had to put in an update for a request earlier. It's been days since I've heard anything. ... It's really not. ... Come again? ... Why was I not told?" Louise stood up with the phone to her ear. She looked set to start smashing things. "This was *two* days ago! Isn't it up to me to judge whether it is connected to the case, not you?" She kicked the chair at her feet. It rolled across the back of the room and stopped at the wall. "If this is how you operate, is it any wonder we have to come up here to hold your hands?"

———

Lookout Corner. If Jake had to describe the discomfort he felt when arriving at a place where his ancestors had buried two dead children, it would go something like this: *A burning sensation. Deep within. In your soul, almost. Do you get what I mean?* Fortunately, he had not planned on explaining this sensation to anyone.

He ran his hands over the plaque on the raised platform: *Captain William Ross, 1710-1765, Just like the Skweda, you will always run through the heart of our town.*

He watched and listened to the water cascade over the

large rock that formed the symbol of Blue Falls. It did little to soothe that burning in his soul.

"J?"

Jake turned and looked down the steps to the raised platform at a squat man with a motorcycle jacket and a long, braided beard ending in beads. Beside him was his antithesis: a tall, suited man with a shaved head, holding a handgun. "Which one is C?"

"Both of us," the squat man replied.

The armed man maintained a glacial expression. He was the muscle, nothing more.

Jake nodded at the squat one. "Well, C-One and"—he nodded at the muscle "C-Two. I was only expecting one of you. However, I'm glad friends were invited, because—"

"They weren't," the biker said.

"Shit, really? Well, I was being presumptuous, then! Meet P."

Peter stepped from the undergrowth with his rifle raised.

The biker turned to see, then regarded Jake with a paling expression.

The muscle stared forward with his gun partially raised.

"Well, say hello, then," Jake said.

"What is this?" C1 asked.

"I want to be on a first name basis." Jake reclined, propping his elbows on the safety bar of the lookout. "More friendly that way."

"I've said no names."

"I used to go to a lot of gatherings in 'Nam that weren't friendly," Peter said. "They never really ended well. Is this one such gathering?"

Jake flitted his eyes to the muscle and read his expression. He was thinking of turning quickly and taking out Peter. "Listen, C-Two, I know what it's like to be the tallest boy in the class, so I'll give you a heads-up I wouldn't normally give. My friend may look as if he's knocking on Heaven's door, but he hasn't shown any signs of slowing down yet."

C_1 instructed C_2 to lower his weapon with a wave of his hand.

C_2 obliged.

"On the ground," Jake said.

The muscle obeyed.

"Name?" Jake asked C_1.

"Keegan."

Clearly, a lie, and one which demonstrated stupidity. "Keegan? Shouldn't you be K then, rather than C? Mind you, my son is taught phonetically at school, and C sounds just like K at the beginning of words, so I can see how you made that mistake."

C_1 glared at him while tugging at a bead on his braided beard.

"I'm Jason," Jake lied. "Notice I used the right letter."

"I thought we were here to do a fucking deal. If so, Keegan will suffice."

"We were here to do a deal, Keegan. Until you brought this goon along."

Keegan gave a display of disbelief by looking back and forth. "As did you?"

"I'm not a goon," Peter said.

Jake saw the muscle's eyelids twitch. He was struggling with the glacial expression he made a living from.

"Listen, Keegan With a C, I have to level with you. I'm not here to do a deal with you. I don't have any product to move. I'm simply here for information."

"Information about what?"

"Another client."

Keegan laughed. He looked at his henchman to join in. Predictably, he didn't. He was too busy trying to keep his death stare intact. "You can't be serious. You might as well let the old vet loose on us. If I tell you about another client, what do you think happens to me?"

"Nothing." Jake drew his arms off the bar. "Because the client you're going to tell me about is a fugitive who has got more important things to worry about than whether Keegan With a C ran his mouth off."

Keegan bit his bottom lip.

"So you know who I'm talking about?"

"What the fuck is this?" Keegan asked.

"Just bad luck on your part. You just took on the wrong client."

"Plain stupidity, if you ask me," Peter said. "Dealing with a chief of police."

Keegan laughed again. "In name only! Have you met the man?"

Jake didn't smile. He stepped forward. "Too many times. It's riddled me with PTSD."

"There's nothing I can tell you. It wasn't me he dealt with."

"Funny that"—Jake drew up close to Keegan—"because your contact details were in his possession."

Keegan nibbled the end of his tongue, then sucked it back in. "I don't know how—"

Jake put a large hand on his shoulder. "Do you know who I am, and why I brought you here, Keegan?"

"No, but it doesn't mat—"

"I'm a Bickford, Keegan."

"The Bickfords are long gone."

Jake smiled. "Many wish it was so. Don't be fooled by

the British accent and the incredible good looks. I'm actually one of those vile fuckers."

"I don't understand why you're telling me this."

Jake nodded at the undergrowth, a stone's throw from where Peter had emerged. "You know what they left here for the town to find."

Keegan nodded. His brow furrowed.

"Now, it just so happens this is your lucky day, Keegan. As a Bickford, I cannot make amends for the despicable things they did, but that won't stop me from trying. That man, Gabriel Jewell, the chief of police—in name only, as you so astutely pointed out—has taken a fourteen-year-old girl. You, I'm assuming, have helped him transport her somewhere. And I am determined, at whatever the cost, to help her."

Keegan shook his head.

Jake tightened his grip on his shoulder. "Do not be mistaken into thinking that my good nature, my desire to help this girl, makes me less of a threat. Please, Keegan, do not be *mistaken*. I have Bickford blood inside me. I am capable of atrocity. I have, in the past, committed atrocity. And a man destined to burn in Hell, does he really have much more to lose? Unless you tell me where you transported Gabriel Jewell and the kidnapped girl, I will kill C-Two. Then I will handcuff you to him and bury you alive with his stiffening body." He pointed at the undergrowth. "Right where my bastard ancestors placed those poor children. So, what'll it be?"

Keegan was grey, but still, he refrained.

"What's it going to be?" Jake said again, raising his voice.

Nothing.

Jake nodded at Peter. "Kill them."

"Okay, *dammit,* wait! I'll tell you, but you won't like it."

"I very rarely like anything I hear these days."

"Our man, the one who took them through the checkpoint—"

"Through the checkpoint? They got through the fucking checkpoint?"

"Yes. But it all went wrong after that."

"How? Why? Where's Gabriel and Kayla? Where are they right now?"

"I don't know. Really, I don't. Let me explain what happened."

———

THREE DAYS BEFORE JAKE PETTMAN LEAVES BLUE FALLS

Gabriel placed his hand over Kayla's mouth.

"What was that?" the officer asked.

"I didn't hear anything," the driver said.

To keep the young girl quiet, Gabriel pressed as hard as he could without crushing her head.

"I need you to step out of your van, sir."

Kayla thrashed, her flailing arms and legs hitting the false wooden van floor above their heads. *Stupid girl.* The car parts were dampening the thuds but remained audible. *Stupid fucking girl.*

"Step out of the vehicle now!"

Gabriel heard the crash of the van door colliding with the officer, followed by a sharp cry of pain.

Kayla writhed.

Gabriel feared she might just break her neck trying to get free of his grip. The compartment was too narrow for him to turn onto his side, so he slid his body at an angle where he could lift his legs onto her.

It steadied her flailing legs, but she still beat on the false floor with a loose fist.

A loud clunk shook the van.

Clunk-clunk-clunk ...

It was obvious to Gabriel that someone was being pummeled against the side of the vehicle. To stand any chance of getting out of this, it needed to be the officer.

Kayla was trying to bite into his palm. She'd stopped punching the false floor and was now clawing at it.

The van door slammed, then the vehicle moved again.

He released Kayla but was then forced to grab her again as the van accelerated.

"Hold on in the back!" the driver shouted so they could hear him over the roaring engine. Missing the warning wouldn't have mattered. Their sudden velocity was warning enough.

As a result of his vicious altercation with Kayla, Gabriel hadn't been bracing himself near the corner of the van as he'd done before, and they both slid backward.

Kayla screamed. She was silenced when their heads cracked against the far end of the hidden compartment.

Wincing against the pain in his crown, Gabriel caught the sound of the sirens far in the distance. Wheels screeched as they were violently thrust against the right side of the van.

Kayla came up on top of him so they were completely wedged between the false floor above and the actual floor below. Gabriel's cheek pressed hard against the side of the van as it completed its sharp turn, then the vehicle straightened. Another sudden burst of acceleration threw Kayla from him, yanked them both back, and rotated them so they were now side on against the far end.

Realizing he was squashing Kayla against the end of the compartment, Gabriel put his palms against them and pushed with all his might. He couldn't contend with the van's movements though, and he felt his elbows buckle. His chest was now crushing her head. "I'm sorry!"

He couldn't hear her response; he doubted she could make one.

Another sharp turn but this one didn't flip them; it just sent them sliding to the left side. Holding onto Kayla, he braced his legs and took the impact for both of them. Gabriel shouted, "Kayla, roll over me. *Now!*"

As the van straightened, Kayla tried to drag herself over him, but the false floor was so low. She became wedged in much the same way she had done during the first turn. As Gabriel predicted, another burst of acceleration forced them both against the end of the compartment again, except, this time, Kayla remained on top of him and so wasn't being crushed.

Gabriel pushed on the false floor to try to create some tension to stop all the sliding. He knew he didn't stand a chance, but his hand brushed against something dangling free—a chain. He traced its path with the sweating fingers of his left hand and realized it was dangling loose around the side of the false floor, potentially from a car part above them. He looped it around his knuckles and tugged. It held. He managed to squeeze his right arm around the small of Kayla's back. "Sorry, this will feel like I'm crushing you again, but there's no other way."

The wheels screeched, and Gabriel felt the almighty pull on his body. The hand he had wrapped in chain burned, and his whole arm felt as if it would be yanked from his body, but he kept them both steady. "Yes!" he whooped as the van straightened. *I've got this sonofabitch—*

The brakes screeched, and the van stopped suddenly with a thud.

The agony in Gabriel's shoulder was unbelievable, but remarkably, he stayed in place.

Kayla, however, was torn from his grasp and vanished into the darkness.

There was a sickening crunch, and the engine died.

9

THE DAY BEFORE JAKE PETTMAN LEAVES BLUE FALLS

LOUISE AND LILLIAN spoke very little as they awaited the call back. Emotions were running high in the office. Not only because they'd just discovered a mechanic named Lance Gage had assaulted an officer and then fled the checkpoint, but also because Louise had recently divulged the devastating truth behind her missing family.

"I could get us both a cup of coffee," Lillian said.

"No," Louise said, leaning forward and rubbing the back of her head; a headache was starting up there.

The phone rang.

"Yes."

"Afternoon, ma'am. I'm Officer Jackson. I handled the situation involving Lance Gage. You asked for a call back?"

"Yes. Why wasn't I notified of the incident?"

"You are looking for Chief Gabriel Jewell and Kayla MacLeoid, I believe? My supervising officer deemed it irrelevant to your investigation."

"*Irrelevant?*" She stood. "Lance Gage assaulted an officer at the checkpoint I requested, then fled arrest! Does it get any more relevant?"

"Ma'am, I can assure you we checked it out. Lance Gage was in custody, and we—"

"Sorry. *Was?*"

"Yes. Lance got bail."

She slammed her fist on the table. "What was he transporting, and where was he going?"

"Rare car parts, for old Porsches and other collectible vehicles. He was heading to the Canadian border. We contacted the company; it all checked out, ma'am."

"He assaulted an officer and fled. How, in any way, does that check out?"

"He has a history of anxiety. He said the officer acted aggressively toward him, and he got spooked."

"And that flimsy excuse was good enough for you?"

"Not really. But Lance will face trial. You can be sure of that, ma'am."

"What does the accused officer have to say?"

"He denies it, of course. But the officer does have some history. A few years back, he was charged with assaulting a prisoner in his custody. The case was dropped eventually, but the damage was kind of done."

"I'm not sure I want to hear all this now, Officer Jackson. A fourteen-year-old girl is in danger."

"Ma'am, Lance Gage had nothing to do with these missing people. The van, which he plowed into a tree, by the way, was clean. He will face the consequences for assaulting one of our officers and evading arrest, but he wasn't smuggling people or drugs."

"Where is the van now?"

"Impounded."

"How thoroughly has it been checked?"

"Thoroughly, I assume."

"You *assume?*"

"Well, there's been no news. That suggests it's fine—"

"Officer! When so much is at stake and someone tells you it's raining, you should go out and check."

"I had a good look myself, at the time. It was full of car parts; nothing else was in there. They would have let me know immediately if there was any contraband in there."

"Officer Jackson, call now to check." She slammed down the phone. The headache had spread into her temples. She massaged them, and said, "I will have a coffee now, please. And see if you can find me some painkillers." The headache was coming on strong, so Louise kept her eyes closed until the phone rang again. "Yes?"

"As I said, ma'am, the van *was* checked out, and there was no contraband, but ..."

Louise opened her eyes. "*But?*"

"Well, ma'am, it's, well ..."

"*Stop* mincing your words, Officer!"

"There was a false floor."

"A false floor!"

"Yes, *but* the compartment was empty. They checked—"

"This is a goddamn circus. Have forensics taken a look?"

"Not sure, *but* it was empty, ma'am. Nobody in there. And no suggestion that anyone had been."

"Did the pursuing officers have sight on the van at *all* times?"

"Let me check. I have the officers' reports here."

Lillian re-entered the room and placed a coffee cup and a packet of Tylenol on the desk.

"Ma'am."

"Yes, officer?"

"You're not going to like this."

"I haven't liked any of this call so far. Cut to the chase."

"They lost sight of him for a few minutes. He took a couple of sharp turns. Eventually, they went back on themselves and found the van hanging off the tree."

"My god. So our fugitive could have been in the compartment?"

"It was a couple of minutes. I think if anyone was in the van, they would have been too hurt to flee."

"Is it possible though, Officer?"

"Well, yes, but—"

"We need Lance Gage back in custody. We need to find out what he was using the compartment for."

"Okay, but I warn you that his lawyer ran a tight ship on his first trip here. Did all his speaking. We couldn't get a word out of him. I don't think he will admit to having any—"

"Just *try*, Officer. It really is the least you can do."

"Okay, ma'am."

"And email over the exact location of the accident."

"Of course, ma'am."

After the phone call, she swallowed two Tylenol with a mouthful of coffee. She eyed Lillian and shook her head. "It doesn't matter how many times I come to these towns, the levels of incompetence never ceases to amaze me." She picked up the phone.

"What now, ma'am?" Lillian asked.

"We get the dogs to the crash site. If Kayla and Gabriel were in that van, we need to find out which way they ran." She slammed her fist on the table. "Two days. Two *fucking* days. We could have had them!"

Keegan rode shotgun.

Peter took the back seat with his rifle at the ready in case the smuggler got any ideas.

The muscle, also known as C2, had been left at lookout point.

"He has some nice views there," Jake said to Keegan. "He can reflect on the choices he's made in life. I hope he decides that working for you hasn't been one of his better ones."

"You really like the sound of your own voice, don't you?" Keegan asked, stroking one of his beaded beard braids.

They stopped by Peter's place for a vehicle changeover. They would have to go through the checkpoint, and having Peter, a well-known face around these parts, at the wheel would cause less fuss. Jake switched to the back seat with the rifle, but before reaching the checkpoint, they pulled over to transfer it into the back of the pickup.

"I've got a license for that," Peter said. "But nowhere on that paper does it say I can point it at the head of pond scum. Damn shame. You best behave."

Keegan said, "Relax, I'm not that low on IQ. I won't be causing any fuss with the law."

"The law!" Jake laughed. "You can use that term loosely around here."

At the checkpoint, the officers greeted Peter without bother but cast a suspicious eye over Jake. Despite already knowing he was in the US legally, they took pleasure in scrutinizing his passport.

"Wasn't my best day in the booth," Jake said.

The officer grunted and handed it back. They weren't too concerned with the biker in the front, but they did give the vehicle a once over and checked Peter's license for the rifle. Eventually, they waved the pickup through.

Jake admired the scenery as Keegan directed Peter down a lane off the beaten track. The trees thickened, and everything became greener. It made him long for home.

After several turns, Keegan instructed them to pull over.

"Get out," Jake said to the biker.

"You guarantee none of this blows back on me?" Keegan asked.

"I'm not guaranteeing anything but use your common sense. A fourteen-year-old girl is in trouble; you're not on anyone's radar."

"Until they've found her?"

"Time for a career change, perhaps?" Peter said. "Now get the fuck out my pickup."

Keegan led them to a large oak tree. "That one."

Jake felt glass crunching underfoot. "They could have cleaned up better." He surveyed the oak tree. "Barely a scratch on it."

"There was on the van," Keegan said. "Written off."

"So, are you giving us the whole story, Keegan?" Jake asked.

"The whole story as I understand it. Lance fed everything back to our lawyer. Our lawyer is a good man."

Peter grunted. "There are no good men smuggling drugs."

"Anything else you can remember?" Jake asked.

"No. I've told you everything. After plowing into this tree, Lance was shaken up, but he's a capable boy. He got into the back and opened the compartment. The girl was unconscious, so your man carried her." He pointed at the woods. "Into there."

"It's been two days," Jake said to Peter. "You reckon you can do it?"

Peter nodded. "When it came to tracking in Vietnam, I was the best."

"You had a dog!"

"Not all the time. Although I don't possess the three hundred million olfactory receptors Prince did, I was tracking long before I had him. Part of the culture, you know? Besides, it hasn't rained in days. I can do this."

Keegan laughed. "You two are insane."

Jake frowned. "Don't know what you're laughing at, gobshite. You've got some tracking of your own to do."

"What do you mean?"

"I mean, the pickup is staying there, and we're going into those trees, which means you're walking home."

"You can't be serious."

Jake raised an eyebrow. "Start walking before I go for the other option."

"Other option?"

Jake nodded at Peter who was taking his rifle from the back of the pickup.

"This is fucked," Keegan said.

"Been saying that ever since I got to Blue Falls. Doesn't help to keep saying it though. Got to do something about it. Go now, Keegan, and you might get to civilization before nightfall."

Peter was already disappearing into the woods. "Come on, then."

―――――――

"Our prey doesn't always act alone," Alpheus said, sliding three brown envelopes down the table.

"More fun to be had," Eli Rook said, reaching for an envelope with his large black hand.

Alpheus circled a dishevelled office belonging to another occupant of the room, Austin Lake, who ran a small store which sold fishing tackle. Austin had closed the shop for the day; after all, the gig Alpheus was currently presenting him with would pay far more handsomely than the loss of a day's takings.

Austin, who looked far too old to be sporting a short mohawk, reached for his envelope with a hand tattooed with Poseidon, God of the Sea, holding a trident, considered by many to be a fish spear.

Autumn Lake, Austin's wife, was young enough to be his daughter. She pushed her envelope away and ran her hand over her husband's mohawk. Chewing, she looked at his profile, then blew a bubble, which popped. "Save your paper. We share."

Alpheus pushed the envelope back toward her. "You do not leave this room without it."

"Big man speak, lady do?" Autumn said, turning to stare up at Alpheus with a large grin.

Autumn had teardrops tattooed on her face. It made Alpheus think of the holes he'd made in Tucker's mother as he drove his hooked beak into her face again and again. He returned her smile. "The envelope."

Also staring at Alpheus, Austin pulled the envelope back toward his wife. "It'll pay for the new boat, baby."

Autumn turned and kissed him on the cheek.

It didn't break Austin's stare. He fixated on Alpheus.

Alpheus smiled again, this time thinking of the eyeball he'd popped between his teeth earlier.

"Keep your woman under control," Eli said. "Some of us round here have more than a new boat to worry about."

Austin turned his eyes on Eli. "Such as?"

"Such as your hospital expenses if you don't get your tattooed ass under control."

Alpheus hissed.

They all looked at him.

"Open the envelopes. The first picture is of the target himself."

"Handsome," Autumn said. She licked her top lip. "Strong."

Austin glared at her, and Eli laughed.

"I can't wait to kill him," Autumn said.

"Psycho bitch," Eli said. "I like it."

"The second photo is of Peter Sheenan," Alpheus continued. "A Vietnam War vet. He lives alone, but according to the information I have been given, he's Jake's closest friend in Blue Falls. They've been getting into mischief together."

"He looks worn out," Eli said. "Not sure I signed up for popping old men."

"You judge by what you see, Eli," Alpheus said. "There are certain fish that play dead, to the extent they take on a blotchy coloration so when the scavenger draws close, it can turn the tables."

Austin nodded.

"We are not in the business of underestimation,"

Alpheus said. He enlightened them on all he'd been told regarding Peter Sheenan, then moved onto the third photograph. "Finally, we have Piper Goodwin. She is in a relationship with Jake Pettman."

"His squeeze," Autumn said with a smile. She turned to Austin and flicked his earlobe with her tongue.

Austin didn't flinch. He just stared at the picture of Piper, unblinking.

"She's a child," Eli said.

"Here, yes," Alpheus said. "It's an old photograph. All I could manage at such short notice."

"Doesn't help if she's changed her hair color?" Eli asked.

Alpheus briefed them on Piper, complete with the revelation: "Biological daughter of Jotham MacLeoid."

Austin sat back, shaking his head. "There are bridges, *many* bridges I would cross, but that really is one much too far."

Alpheus nodded. "Normally, you'd be right to be prudent, Austin. But the MacLeoid empire is no more, so this changes nothing."

"Make me believe that," Austin said.

"My business is not to make you believe anything. My business is to hunt and kill. I can go singular, or I can go plural; both offer interesting opportunities."

Eli hammered the table with his fists and grinned. "Hell, I'm in!"

Austin stared at Alpheus; he still looked far from convinced.

Autumn leaned over and whispered. It was a show. Everyone could hear what she was saying. "Easy pickings. Birdman is completely insane. We will barely have to break a sweat."

Keeping his eyes fixated on Alpheus, he nodded. "Okay, so what's the plan?"

"Cooperation." Alpheus circled the room to the other side of the table. "Contrary to popular belief, hawks can hunt together, especially when it comes to hunting larger prey. One hawk flies in and causes a panic flurry of retreat, driving the prey into the talons of the second hawk."

"I think you need to recount. There's four of us," Autumn said with a wink. "Doesn't sound like you have a lot of faith in our abilities?"

"The intel I have on Jake Pettman just requires more caution than normal. This situation will work. We will cause panic, draw him out, then we will execute. The rewards are more than generous."

10

**THREE DAYS BEFORE JAKE PETTMAN
LEAVES BLUE FALLS**

A S THE DAY died, Gabriel carried the girl he loved deeper into the woods.

She woke a few times, looked up at his face, whimpered, then sought solace back in sleep.

It pained Gabriel to see how much he repulsed her.

She'd hit her head quite hard when the van had plowed into that tree. He didn't know how bad the injury was. He could be taking an almighty gamble with her life.

Earlier in this trek, he'd stopped to assess their open wounds. The knife wound Molly had administered hurt to hell, but the bleeding didn't seem to have worsened, so he left the bandage in place. He dry-swallowed some painkillers and chased it down with a couple of Adderall for good measure. He hoped it would give clarity to a situation he'd lost control of. He didn't expect to get any. After all, what the hell was he supposed to do now that his plan had failed?

Kayla's bullet wound delivered, to his shame, by him had still been leaking. He didn't have a clean bandage though, so he simply removed the bloody one, cast it into the undergrowth, and tied the wound in the sling she'd been using. She had grimaced and moaned throughout the experience but was too out of it to fight off his attempts at playing nursemaid.

Throughout the journey, he'd been using the direction of the sun to keep on a northern trajectory. That would take him to the River Skweda. He had no idea how long the journey would be, but if he could make it there, he believed he had one last card to play.

Kayla moaned in his arms. In the dying light, her face darkened and lost the glow and freshness he so adored in her young skin. He laid her down and sat on an overturned tree to catch his breath.

She opened her eyes and stared up at him. This time, she didn't whimper or slip back away. "Where are we?"

Gabriel surveyed the gnarled oaks that closed in on them and the canopy overhead, which flickered as the sun completed its descent. Sensing the approach of twilight, the insects were kicking up a racket around them. "In the woods."

"I don't understand. I remember the van." She started to cry. "It was dark and horrible and ... and ..."

Gabriel fell to his knees and placed a large hand on her good arm. "It's over now."

"My head. It hurts."

"We crashed. I'm sorry."

"I dreamed about my father, my brother. I dreamt I was safe ... with them."

"You were never safe with them."

She didn't respond. She just closed her eyes. "I just want to go back to sleep."

He watched the tears roll down her face as the light continued to die. He smelled burning and stood to look around. "Can you smell that, Kayla?"

She didn't respond.

He turned full circle again and caught the small glow of a fire not too far in the distance. "Look!"

Still no response.

He bent down to swoop her up, grimacing over the pain in his wounded arm. As he crunched through the undergrowth, the sun finalized its descent, giving the fire a bolder appearance in the murky evening; the noise of crackling, spitting wood intensified, and the sounds of insects dissipated. Gabriel entered a wide clearing.

Someone was sitting on a rock with their back to them, tending to a fire, which wasn't as brazen as Gabriel had first believed. The individual had built a tripod over the flames by binding together three long pieces of wood. A steaming pot hung from a rope attached to the center.

Pushed farther back from the campfire was a small log cabin. Its moss-covered roof stretched over the front door, which was being propped up by two misshapen beams of wood. A brick chimney was attached to the side.

Kayla was conscious now, so he allowed her down.

"Remember," Gabriel whispered to her, "remember what happened to Molly. Please, not again."

Kayla didn't respond, but he was confident she wouldn't say anything. Putting that grotesque driver in danger by shouting was one thing, endangering the life of this innocent person was another.

The person who tended the fire and presumably owned the cabin was yet to turn.

A shiver ran down Gabriel's spine as he acknowledged for the first time that he was unarmed, having opted to leave Molly's cumbersome shotgun at her place. "Hello?"

A middle-aged woman with gray-streaked, long black hair turned toward them. She wore cargo pants and a thick, frayed green jumper.

"Do you live out here?" Gabriel asked.

She smiled. "Of course." Her crackling, hoarse voice suggested she'd spent too much time hovering over smoking campfires. "Look at you two! I can't remember last time someone stopped by."

"Please. We need some water and food if possible."

"Is this your daughter?"

Gabriel nodded.

Despite age being on her side, the woman groaned as she stood and partially unfolded her hunched back. Using a walking stick, she hobbled toward them. As she neared, she had eyes only for Kayla. "Well, aren't you a pretty thing?"

"Thank you," Kayla said.

The woman struggled as she came right up to them, so Gabriel expected her face to be heavily lined, for her to look older than he'd originally anticipated. Surprisingly, she was younger.

She put her hand to Kayla's face.

It made Gabriel's heart heavy when he saw Kayla didn't flinch, as she always did when he touched her.

"Such a delightful face." The woman stroked her cheek. "So, so beautiful."

"Thank you," Kayla said.

"But so tired and pale."

"Yes. We're thirsty and hungry," Gabriel said, trying to pull her prying eyes from Kayla. "Can you help us?"

The woman turned her smile to Gabriel. "Of course ..." She squinted at him. "Do I know you from somewhere?"

"I wouldn't think so. We're from out of town."

"Really, I never forget a face."

"Impossible, I'm sorry. This is our first time here. I'm Bryan, and this is my daughter Cecile. We went for a walk in the woods and got lost. Stupid, really."

"Not so much stupid, as *unusual*. This has never happened before, and I never really expected it to." A hiss sounded from behind them. "Dammit, the stew!"

"Let me," Gabriel said. He sprinted to the tripod over the fire.

"Thank you. You may have noticed I'm not too nimble on my feet."

The fire packed some punch. He winced as he slipped a stick through the handle of the steaming pot, hoisted it free, and laid it flat on some rocks.

"A pickup ran me down when I was seventeen."

"I'm sorry to hear that." Gabriel looked into the pot at the thick stew, feeling hunger pangs.

"Woke up with my bottom half twisted the wrong way. I was told I would never walk again."

Gabriel turned to face her. "How long have you been living out here?"

"Since I proved them all wrong. A decade or so."

"What's your name, ma'am?"

"I'm Susannah Gott." She waved him away. "But enough about me. How did you hurt your arm, Bryan?"

"I fell, before, over a dead tree, cut myself on the branches."

Susannah turned to Kayla and pressed her hand to her

123

face again. "And you, Cecile dear, how did you hurt yourself?"

Kayla spoke without hesitation. "The same way."

Gabriel closed his eyes and forced back a groan. It sounded too coincidental. "Well, I fell into Kayla, and she went over with me," Gabriel said, trying to rescue the situation. "Curse of being so big, I guess."

"Well," Susannah said, "nobody has ever come to me in need out here. I appreciate the opportunity. Let's go inside and get you nourished." She stroked her cheek again. "Such a beautiful face."

The log cabin was comprised of one larger room with two smaller rooms attached. Considering Susannah had been here for over a decade, the place was rather sparsely decorated. The centerpiece was the hearth beneath the chimney.

"Why not cook there?" Gabriel asked.

"A nest in the chimney. Haven't the heart to move them on until the fledglings have grown."

A long table was lined with spidery candelabras bereft of candles.

"Please guests, sit," Susannah said. Her eyes hadn't moved from Kayla since the moment they'd agreed to come inside.

Did she suspect something? To be fair, who wouldn't? Two strangers stumbling onto your property in the middle of nowhere with bloody wounds? He wondered if he should have carried in that stick he'd used to take the pot from the fire. However, as he watched Susannah grimace and groan as she hobbled around the table, he realized he had little to fear.

"My cellphone has no reception out here," Gabriel lied. "Do you have a phone?"

"Yes, in the back, beside the desktop hooked up to the internet."

"Really?"

"No!" Susannah laughed. "When I opted to get out of the world, I opted not to bring it with me!"

Gabriel nodded. "I see."

As Gabriel sat, he scanned the bare log walls. He considered suggesting a watercolor or two to bring the place to life but kept himself in check. Offending his hostess wasn't in his best interests right now. "Is there a Mr. Gott?" Gabriel asked, pulling out a chair so Kayla could sit beside him.

"Of course not." Susannah put two glasses of water on the table, then pressed Kayla's hand around her glass. "Drink, Cecile dear. You must be thirsty."

"I am," Kayla said, waiting for the lingering hand to move so she could drink.

"Hydration is the key to good skin." Susannah lifted her hand and let her knuckles brush Kayla's cheek. "Drink, please. Drink as much as you need."

Before, Gabriel had carried the pot into the cabin and laid it by her sink. Now, using her walking stick, Susannah limped to it to spoon the steaming stew into two bowls.

"How often do you go into town?" Gabriel asked.

"I go for supplies once a month."

"Blue Falls?"

"Sharon's Edge."

"Ah, when we planned this trip, we opted for Blue Falls."

"The nicest of three not particularly nice places."

"We like it. Since Cecile's mother, Jane, died five years back, we've been on annual walking trips to different location in New England."

"The walking around here is nice." Susannah hobbled slowly over with the bowls on a tray.

"Yes," Gabriel said. "If you don't get lost in the woods and injure yourself!"

Susannah nodded as she laid down the tray and slid it toward them. "We will see what we can do about re-dressing the wounds after you eat." She nodded at one of the rooms at the back. "I have some medical supplies."

Gabriel lifted the first bowl and placed it in front of Kayla.

She nodded in gratitude but had resumed keeping her head down and avoiding eye contact with anyone. After taking her first mouthful, Gabriel reached for his bowl.

"Rabbit," Susannah said.

"It smells great." Gabriel lifted the spoon to his lips and paused as he recalled Molly's chowder and relived the moment when the world had tilted, and everything had collapsed into chaos. He eyed Susannah—a troubled recluse living with life-changing injuries. She wasn't aware of what was really happening here. They were perfectly safe. The food was perfectly safe. He only realised how hungry he was when he spooned it into his mouth, then ate quickly.

"Looks like you two stumbled on me at just about the right time."

Gabriel nodded as he ate.

Susannah sat opposite them, without a bowl.

Gabriel swallowed a mouthful. "Not eating?"

"If there's any left. I want you to eat until you are full."

"That's kind. But please, eat."

Susannah smiled. "I've made up my mind." She turned to watch Kayla for quite some time with a glazed expression.

When Kayla finished, she said, "Thank you, ma'am."

Susannah smiled again. "You're welcome, my beautiful girl. So very welcome."

Although it was peculiar, Kayla welcomed the attention Susannah gave her. The hand on the face, the fingers on her hand, and the smile as she ate gave her some reassurance that she wasn't completely alone with this madman. It hadn't been this way for so very long—months locked in his basement while he masturbated at her door, watching her brother bleed out in front of her, sealed in the trunk of his car as he drove recklessly, tied up in a farmhouse where two innocent people were murdered, and finally, crushed and manhandled by him in a compartment beneath a transit van, with no one to tell of her experiences.

No one to *help*.

Until now.

The kind, injured lady who cannot take her eyes off me.

She was the one. She just had to be.

"I need the bathroom," Kayla said.

"Of course, Cecile dear," Susannah said, standing.

As Kayla stood, she noticed Gabriel had fixated on her with narrowed eyes as he drank from a glass of water. His eyes spoke volumes. *Molly. Remember Molly.*

Yes, I remember, you bastard. She almost had you though, didn't she? Someone will stop you. I know they will.

She felt Susannah's hand slip into hers. "Come this way."

Susannah escorted her to one of two doors leading off the main room. Kayla was glad of the support; she still felt disorientated from the head injury.

"The little girl's room." Susannah turned Kayla to face her and wiped the corner of the girl's mouth with her thumb. "Gosh, you were hungry. See that you wash, Cecile dear. We don't want a single mark on such a perfect face. I'll wait here for you to finish. I also feel the call of nature."

Kayla entered the bathroom and closed the door. She had no plan. *No clue.* Her heart thrashed in her chest. *Susannah.* Her one hope. But how? *How?*

Like the rest of the cabin, the bathroom was small and basic—an old metal tub for bathing in, a toilet with no cover, a bathroom mirror, and a sink with a toothpaste holder.

An idea came to her. A *desperate* idea. However, *if* she wanted an end to this, *if* she wanted to live, she had to act. She went to the sink and popped the cap on the toothpaste. She lifted the nozzle to the mirror. A voice screamed in her head, *You're insane! You'll get yourself and Susannah killed! He'll see it!* The stew rose up the back of her throat. It tasted more acidic than it had done going down.

Susannah had said, "I also feel the call of nature." She was coming in next and could clean it off. It felt like the right move. She squeezed the toothpaste and wrote on the mirror. Afterward, she washed her face with cold water and dried it on the hand towel. She opened the bathroom door and sidestepped Susannah, who disappeared into the bathroom.

"Is everything okay?" Gabriel asked as she sat beside him.

She nodded. She didn't dare speak in case she vomited the stew burning her throat.

"Good. Remember, this is for the best. She must have a

vehicle somewhere if she goes into town. I'm guessing there's a road close by here. We *need* her to help us. I know she's weird, but you must keep your mouth closed. If she wants to touch you, let her touch you. I know it seems rather intense, but it is a necessary evil."

Kayla looked at him. *Rather her than you, fucker.*

The bathroom door opened.

Gabriel drank from the glass while Kayla chanced a look back at their hostess.

Susannah was standing there, smiling.

Had she read her words? HELP ME! written as neatly as she could with toothpaste?

Still grinning, Susannah raised a finger to her lips.

11

THE DAY BEFORE JAKE PETTMAN LEAVES BLUE FALLS

"NOW WHAT THE merry hell is going on here?" Eli asked Alpheus from the passenger seat.

"It's a checkpoint." Alpheus checked his rearview mirror to ensure his other two soldiers, Autumn and Austin, were still cruising close behind.

"That's fairly obvious, Bird. I'm asking about the cause of said checkpoint."

"It's unrelated to our business."

"Anything related to Blue Falls at this time is surely related to our business."

"The chief of police kidnapped a little girl. This is their attempt to hem him in."

"And you knew about this, Bird?"

"I did. And that's twice you've addressed me by my

surname. It seems prudent to warn you now, Eli, that you may not survive a third time."

Eli grimaced, regarded Alpheus, and laughed. "Wow. You're one funny man ..." He broke off, having clearly decided not to opt for a third go.

"Jesus, why are you slowing?" Eli asked. "The checkpoint is for the other direction, and they've not made any signal for us to stop. Our luck has come in!"

Alpheus stopped.

"A car full of weaponry and you stop to chat to the boys in blue?" Eli asked.

"Ignorance is dangerous, Eli."

"Ignorance keeps us out of prison."

"And to be visible is to be invisible."

Eli elbowed the door. "Shit, I knew I shouldn't have answered your call after last time."

Alpheus lowered the window and waved over a young officer.

The officer relished the attention, standing upright and puffing out his chest when he arrived at Alpheus's window.

"Are we okay to come through, Officer?"

"Yes, sorry, sir. No one pulled you over. Our focus is mainly on vehicles heading in the other direction."

"Someone trying to run from you, Officer?"

"Something like that, sir." The officer stepped backward from the window.

"If we had our way, we'd never leave Blue Falls; we love it here. We come here to hunt once a year."

The officer smiled. "You and ...?" He knelt and looked in the vehicle.

Eli offered him a smile and a wave with his large black hand.

The officer's smile fell away. Racism was as thick in the air as midges in summer in this part of the world.

"My brother," Alpheus said.

"Brother?"

"Adopted."

"I see, and the car behind?"

"Our friends. Married. They own a gun smithery to the north. We are here to hunt and are fully licensed. Would you like to see our papers?"

"That won't be necessary. Just register at the station, sir."

"Not here?" Alpheus asked with a smile.

The officer grinned. "I appreciate you trying to save time, sir, but we prefer it if you just use the station."

"Will do. Who are you trying to catch, by the way?" Alpheus lifted his two gloved hands from the wheel to gesture catching something. "Is it dangerous to head into Blue Falls now?"

The officer shook his head. "No. We got this. Just drive safely, sir." He tapped the roof of the car. "Have a pleasant stay."

"Will do."

As they drove away, Eli said, "You're insane."

"No. Just invisible."

———

"Ma'am?" Lillian said.

Louise leaned against the back of Peter Sheenan's pickup with her head lowered slightly and her hands clenched.

"Ma'am?" Lillian put a hand on the tall lieutenant's back.

She drew away sharply before Lillian could make contact. "How? Answer me that, Officer! How?"

"I don't know."

"Really? You said he was resourceful back at the station."

"He is."

"That suggests to me that you know how he operates!"

"I'm sorry, ma'am. I've not been in touch with him since you asked him in for help."

Louise slammed the palm of her hand against the side of the pickup. "Shit! This is my fault. I'm taking him in for obstructing justice."

Lillian felt her stomach turn. "With all due respect, ma'am, he's not obstructing it; he's trying to usher it along."

"If"—Louise shook a finger—"if I discover he has lifted evidence from somewhere, then that is obstruction. How else did they get here before us? They must have found something at the farmhouse."

Barking dogs distracted Lillian. She saw a small group of armed officers lingering at the forest's edge with two search dogs pulling at their leads.

"They're ready!" an officer called out.

"I'm coming too!" Louise replied.

One of her own officers from the MSP stepped forward. "That really isn't necessary, ma'am. We can handle it." He held up the bulky long-range walkie-talkie. "I will stay in constant contact."

Louise checked the firearm in her holster. "I'm coming." She turned to Lillian. "Back to the station, Officer. I need someone there I can trust. I've requested the helicopters, but they will struggle through the treetops, especially in the dark, so they'll probably wait for first light." She handed over the walkie-talkie. "Keep me updated."

Jake checked his watch. They'd been trekking for well over an hour. With each step, his confidence ebbed away that little bit more. Every time Peter paused to examine the undergrowth and surmise the direction to proceed, Jake held his tongue. His negative thoughts wouldn't help. If he took away Peter's belief too, he'd be taking away their final hope.

When Jake observed the beginning of the sun's descent, he stifled a groan. Rather than mention the fact that tracking in the dark would be a tall order, he focused on an insect bite and scratched it so hard that it bled.

"*Jake!*"

Jake ran to where Peter was kneeling. "Yes?"

Peter held up a bloody rag. It was bittersweet. They were heading in the right direction, but someone could be injured. "Let's hope it's his," Peter said.

"The road accident. Kayla could be in a bad way."

"We can't think like this. Let's pick up the pace, Jake. They're heading north."

"How do you know?"

"It's been obvious to me for a while now, which has made this a lot easier than it looks."

"You're a wonderful man, Peter."

"Shame I didn't just record that."

"Record what? I didn't say anything."

Peter sighed. "Precisely."

Peter led them north for thirty more minutes while Jake resisted the urge to tear his arms apart.

"They like British blood up this way," Peter said.

"Who? The insects or the locals?"

Peter didn't respond. He'd stopped walking a couple

yards ahead of Jake and was looking around. "What the hell?"

Jake came out into a clearing beside him. "A log cabin?"

"Out here? Talk about getting away from it all."

Jake was already running toward it.

"Shouldn't we be more careful?" Peter called after him.

Following his grisly discoveries at Molly Holbrook's farmhouse, Jake was through with the stealthy, safety-first approach. Adrenaline was riding too high for that now, especially since the discovery of the bloody rag. "Cover me," Jake said as he charged up the steps and pounded on the door.

Nothing.

He tried again. "Is anyone home?" he asked loudly.

After one last try, and with still no response, he went through the unlocked door, half-expecting to see the bodies of the poor residents strewn in pieces over the cabin floor. Instead, he found only emptiness.

Peter drew alongside him with his rifle at the ready. "Eerie."

Jake circled the bare room, noticing two bowls on the table, another bloody rag beside the sink, and an old, walking stick propped against the first of two closed doors leading into the back.

Peter said, "I still got you covered if—"

Jake didn't wait for Peter to finish, never mind ready himself; he was through the back door into a small bedroom, which was almost completely taken up by a queen-sized bed.

"Jesus, Jake!" Peter said.

"I'm through tiptoeing," Jake said, scanning the dishevelled bed and noticing a large blood stain on one of

135

the pillows. "Something happened here." He held up the pillow at the open bedroom door to show Peter.

"Could be a nosebleed."

"Could be, but probably isn't." Jake slipped past Peter for the second room—a bathroom. He moved in close to a smashed bathroom mirror. He saw traces of blood in the spiderweb of cracks. In the tub were yet more bloody rags. "Someone is definitely worse for wear."

"We've missed them again."

Jake nodded at Peter. He had a thought. "Outside." He flew back through the cabin, down the porch steps, and circled to the back.

Peter trailed close behind him to a small hut, approximately three yards wide. It looked sturdier and far less worn than the log cabin.

Jake approached the door.

"I don't like it," Peter said.

"What's to like?"

"Jesus. That's not what I meant, and you know it! I'm talking about the risk you're putting yourself in. At least give a warning first!"

"Anyone in there?" Jake asked loudly.

No answer.

"Satisfied?"

"No." Jake grabbed the handle and noticed the splintering around the frame. The door wasn't even closed, having been forced open by someone. "Something's happened here."

The door swung open with the gentlest of pulls.

Jake winced. A pungent chemical smell saturated the air. The floor was drenched and strewn with vials and bottles, some of which had smashed. He moved carefully into the hut, unable to avoid the acrid fluids but swerving the bigger pieces of broken glass. He scanned the walls, and his breath died in his throat. He stumbled backward toward the door, no longer concerned about the glass. "Jesus Christ!"

Peter's hands were on him, trying to steady him.

"No!"

"What's wrong?"

"No, no, *no!*"

"More dead bodies?"

"Worse." Jake pulled away from Peter and leaned against the side of the log cabin, fighting a need to vomit.

While staring at the remains of a campfire, Jake heard the crack of a branch behind him.

"It's me," Peter said.

"What kind of fucked-up world do we live in?" Jake asked, still staring down.

Peter sucked in a deep breath. "The kind of fucked-up world where shit like that happens."

"I've seen bad things in my time, Peter, very bad things, but that—*that*—how can anyone will themselves on after such atrocity?"

"It's hard," Peter said, kneeling. "After Vietnam, I thought my ticket was up. But there is a way back because that hell wasn't everything. Regardless of how it may seem right now, the world isn't just shadows. Look around them."

"Not sure I can."

"See Piper. See your son."

Jake sighed, shook his head, and turned. "Are you telling me to pull myself together?"

"Yes, but there is no need to, really."

"Ah, and why not?"

"Because you will, Jake. You will because you always do. You're one of life's soldiers."

Jake looked back in the direction of the hut. "I need to contact Lillian. They need to know what's here."

"We have no reception."

"Well, we can't go back now."

"No, we can't. Not when we're so close. Because we are, you know."

"How do you know?"

"The ashes of this campfire are still warm, Jake. In fact, if you look close enough, you can just about see the dying embers."

12

**THREE DAYS BEFORE JAKE PETTMAN
LEAVES BLUE FALLS**

W HEN SUSANNAH offered her bed for the night,
Gabriel, at first, refused, but not because he didn't
want to stop for the night. After all, they were exhausted
following the van accident and the gruelling trek through
the woods. He refused because he couldn't trust himself
lying in bed alone with Kayla.

Susannah, the kindest albeit strangest of hostesses,
persisted, and eventually, Gabriel found his willpower
eroded to the point that he'd nodded in agreement.
Susannah said she'd get some rest in a separate hut around
the back.

After leaving Susannah to put away the dishes, he
closed the door and turned to Kayla. "You did well."

Without replying, Kayla moved quickly around to the
other side of the queen-sized bed.

Again, he felt a sadness deep inside over the fact he had such a profoundly negative effect on her. "I know how scared and tired you are. I appreciate it must have been difficult not to say anything."

Kayla nodded but still didn't respond. At one point, in his basement, she'd been a rather feisty young lady who had voiced her opinion on several occasions. These recent events were knocking it out of her. This wasn't what he wanted; it was the fiery young lady he'd fallen for.

Gabriel gestured at the old chair in the corner. "You don't have to worry. I'll sleep in the chair. You can have the bed."

She regarded him, curiously, like someone who'd spent their lives in a cave and were only now beholding fellow man for the first time.

"I won't touch you." *Not until you are ready.* It was a promise he'd made to himself—a promise he'd struggled over the past months to keep but one he was willing to fight for now with every ounce of his being.

Fully dressed, she climbed into bed.

He sat in the chair and watched her desperately fidget as she struggled for comfort. The wound he'd opened in her arm the guilty party.

While she fought for sleep, he pulled the Adderall bottle from his pocket and emptied the nine remaining pills into his palm. *Everything comes to an end.* He counted out three pills and dropped the rest into the bottle. He stared at the three pills as his hand shook, such was the desperation for the high they offered. *But then what?* He'd be down to six and running dangerously low with no idea how much of this journey remained. He replaced them in the bottle. Taking them before an evening's rest would be a waste of that explosion of clarity and vigor and would surely affect his sleep.

He spent some time thinking about Collette, the sister he'd adored as a child. He imagined, as he so often did, stopping her leaving the house on the day she had taken her last journey to the Mason general store.

"Let me go," he said in the fantasy. "I'll get Father's lighter."

Would he have found his way to the bottom of the River Skweda instead then?

Probably.

Did he care?

Not one bit.

He cried gently in the chair as the night passed, and only when he heard Kayla's gentle snoring did he masturbate.

Day was only just breaking when Gabriel awoke. His first instinct was to check that Kayla was still there.

Lying on her back with hair covering half of her face, she looked both gentle and beautiful.

Thud.

It came from around the back of the cabin. He wondered if this is what had woken him.

Thud.

Recalling what Susannah had said the previous night about sleeping in a hut around the back, he rose from his chair. He stretched, listening to his stiff spine crack, passed wind, and exited the bedroom.

Thud.

The smell of yesterday's stew teased him on the way

through the living room. He'd certainly not eaten his fill the previous evening. She'd been cooking for one, and the portion sizes had been relatively small.

Thud.

Outside in sunlight, he became acutely aware of how groggy he was. Yes, he'd just woken up, but this was *heavy* disorientation. Withdrawal? Was his body calling for amphetamines?

Thud.

He circled the cabin until he could see the small hut. It looked newer than the log cabin. The door stood wide open. He approached and saw Susannah to his left splitting logs with an axe. *Really? Was this a dream? The woman could barely move the night before.*

She bent to ready another log, stood, lined up the axe, drew it back, and swung it in a perfect arc.

Thud. The log split perfectly in two.

"Feeling better today?" he asked.

She flashed him a smile and readied another log.

There was a big difference between someone acting peculiar and just outright lying, and Gabriel was in no mood for deception. He stepped toward her. "I said, are you feeling better?"

"Yes." She lined up another log.

"Last night you were struggling to walk, and today you are swinging an axe like a seasoned woodcutter."

She looked back at him. "A night with my trophies does that for me. It *invigorates*."

"Trophies?"

"Take a look." Susannah nodded toward the hut. "In there." She swung the axe.

Thud

He kept a distance from the odd woman to prevent the

flailing axe from inadvertently striking him, then headed to the cabin door.

"How's that beautiful daughter of yours? Such an adorable little face!"

He entered the cabin, expecting to see a makeshift bedroom—a mattress on the floor perhaps, or at least a sofa to rest upon. He saw neither. What he saw and smelled was only death. "Jesus." He stared in horror at the wall strewn with bottles and surgical equipment above tables. He stumbled several steps and was forced to steady himself against one of the tables.

Thud.

Six faces had been carved from their victims, from the scalp to the top of the neck, before being attached to mounts. The pins stretched the flesh so the black hollows of the eye sockets were wide and yearning. Their foreheads and chins were also pulled taut into triangular points, making the age of these poor victims indeterminable. A leathery look to the skin suggested they had either been cured in salt or perhaps a chemical from the table before him.

Thud.

With a hand to his mouth, tasting last night's stew, Gabriel backpedalled. He staggered over a creased Welcome mat, but his hand found the frame of the open door before he could topple backward.

Thud.

Sudden pressure on his hand. *Blinding pain.* He snapped his hand away and threw himself into a turn.

Susannah was there, holding her axe.

He let himself stumble backward before she could split him in half with it. The pain in his left hand was excruciating. He held it up and saw that the tops of his

143

forefinger and middle finger were missing. Blood spewed from the cleaved digits. "Fuck!"

She swung the axe again.

He leapt backward and landed on a bottle-covered table. He heard the wood splinter and crack beneath his bodyweight. He landed on the floor and heard the glass follow, smashing around him. He felt the loose chemicals soaking into his trousers. He looked up to see Susannah closing in with the axe raised, so he drew back his foot and planted it into one of her knees.

She lurched backward. When she caught the creased mat that had almost uprooted Gabriel, she flew backward through the door and landed on her backside.

Knowing this was his only opportunity, Gabriel tried desperately to get to his feet, but when he put his injured hand to the ground and it contacted the chemicals, he roared in agony. Trying to get himself to his feet with his good hand was also a problem, because he was now sliding all over the place in the fluid and the debris. "Shit! Shit!" Eventually, he managed to get himself over to the wall and, with his good hand, started to work his way back up.

But Susannah had also regained her footing. She hovered in the doorway. Her eyes were wide, and her breathing hissed through bared, clenched teeth.

Gabriel bent to grab a jagged table leg with his good right hand. He held it in her direction to show her he was more than capable of wielding it. "Come on, you sick fucker! Make it a good one, or I'll stake you through the heart."

She lifted her foot and held it over the threshold, teasing him.

Gabriel gritted his teeth. He flipped the table leg in his

hand so he held it like a spear. With his damaged hand, he gestured for her to come. "Let's go."

She shook her head, stepped backward, and slammed the door.

He heard the lock turn. "You think that'll keep me in?"

"Keep an eye on him, my children," she called through the door. "I'm going to get Daddy's pop gun."

Gabriel cast the chair leg to one side and, taking care not to fall foul of the mat again, charged and buried his right shoulder into the door. The wind was knocked from his body, and the entire hut shook around him. The door barely shifted. He lined himself up for a second barge and roared when he made contact. This time he heard splintering. It took him three more barges to burst free of the hut. He was fortunate to keep his footing, but even more fortunate to be still alive when Susannah pulled that trigger. Wood chippings from the hut peppered his face.

Susannah was coming quickly, readying another shot.

He turned and sprinted alongside the hut. Another bang sounded. This time, the wood chippings came from a tree.

"Come back!" Susannah roared.

Fuck you, Gabriel thought, diving into the woods. He ran for quite some time. A couple more shots rang out, but none seemed to come close. When he was certain she'd given up the chase, he collapsed out of breath and stared wide-eyed at his ruined hand.

———

Kayla was relieved to see Susannah enter the bedroom with the rifle and a small, cool box hanging by a strap over one shoulder. "It's over, dear. He fought, but I got the better of him."

Tears sprang in Kayla's eyes.

Susannah propped the rifle against the wall and hobbled to the foot of the queen-sized bed. She paused midway to catch her breath, with her head lowered.

"Thank you," Kayla said, rubbing her eyes. "Thank you so much."

Susannah looked up and caught Kayla's stare. "It must be a relief, Cecile dear?"

"It's not Cecile. He lied. It's Kayla."

"I see." Susannah came around to the side of the bed, slipped the strap off her shoulder, and, with the cool box on her lap, sat on the edge. Susannah regarded her with eyes full of sympathy. "If you want to tell me what happened to you, I'm listening. If you don't, I understand completely."

"I just want to go home." Her voice broke, and the tears came again. *There is no home, Kayla. He took that away from you. Your father, your brother, the farm. Everything.*

"There, there, Kayla dear." Susannah stroked her face. "You don't deserve what happened to you. No one does. But especially you. You have such beautiful skin."

"He told me he loved me. He *kept* telling me."

"Maybe he did, in his own twisted way."

"I'm so glad he's dead. It is over, isn't it?"

Susannah smiled. "Oh, it's over. You have my word on that." She looked ahead. "All over." She unzipped the cool box on her lap without looking down at it. "And now, we need to get you back to the land of the living, don't we?"

"Yes. It's just, well, I don't really have anywhere to go anymore. He killed Ayden, my brother. He was all I had left."

"You poor thing. You know you're welcome to stay with

me for as long as you need. I know it's the middle of nowhere." She stroked Kayla's face again while reaching into the cool box. "But you wouldn't be the first long-term guest I've had. I would treat you very well. I treat them all so very well."

"Thank you, but I'd really like to get back to Blue Falls. I have a friend, Cody. His mother, Jenna, worked for my father. I think they would help me."

"Your wish, my darling girl, is my command. But first, we must do something about the wound on your arm. How's it feeling?"

"It hurts."

"I'm not surprised, Kayla dear." She nodded at the bandage. "It looks like it's been bleeding quite heavily. You need to be taking antibiotics for a deep cut like that. I bet that mean man said nothing."

"I'm sure Jenna will take me to the hospital."

"I'm sure she will, but fortunately for you, we can get a head start." Susannah pulled a syringe from the cool box. "We don't want to risk sepsis, do we?"

Kayla shook her head. "I'll be fine, Susannah, thank you. I hate needles. I'd rather—"

"Don't be ridiculous, precious." She reached out to stroke her face again. "Your skin is hot, Kayla dear. Yes, you've been crying, but I cannot risk an infection on my watch. Who knows what nasty bacteria you picked up out in those woods."

Alarm bells started to ring. Yes, she would always be grateful to Susannah for saving her, but she wasn't the most stable woman she'd ever met; she had chosen to live in the middle of the woods all alone, for a start. Was there really need for an injection right now? She'd prefer the hospital to look first. "Thanks, but I really do have a thing about—"

Susannah clenched her wrist. "Don't be ridiculous, dear."

Kayla's constant fear, which had been momentarily alleviated, flared again. "Please ... I hate needles."

"I used to be a veterinarian once upon a time. So many sensitive, gentle creatures. *Beautiful creatures.* You won't feel a thing, I promise."

"No, thank you." Kayla tugged her wrist back, but Susannah's grip tightened.

"You are being ridiculous, Kayla dear."

Kayla shook her head and tugged harder.

Susannah slid the needle into her wrist and hit the plunger.

Kayla yanked her arm, but Susannah's grip was unyielding; for a woman who looked so weak and damaged by a road accident, she was incredibly strong. A sudden dizziness kicked in. And with that came the cold realization that she was not yet out of the woods—figuratively as well as literally.

"There, dear. You'll feel better soon."

"What have you given me?" she asked, but it felt as if someone else had asked it now.

"That beauty you have is a rarity. I am going to honor you, Kayla dear." Susannah slipped a scalpel from the cool box. "Sleep now, knowing that special gift you have will live forever."

Kayla slept.

13

THE DAY BEFORE JAKE PETTMAN LEAVES BLUE FALLS

ALPHEUS LED HIS soldiers to the parking lot near the summit of Ross Hill.

Autumn and Austin Lake pulled alongside them.

He nodded at Eli in the passenger seat. "Get in the car with them."

Eli looked out the window at the car, then back at Alpheus. "You want me to spend the night in the car with the lovebirds?"

Alpheus nodded.

Eli looked back at the couple who were in a passionate embrace. "For fuck's sake! You sure we can't go for a motel? Actually, forget it. I remember ..." He rolled his eyes. "We swoop in, and we swoop out!" Eli stepped from the vehicle and leaned back in. "You sure this is the way you want to play it, Bi—" The memory of Alpheus's threat at the checkpoint stopped him just in time.

"The plan is based on instinct," Alpheus said without looking at Eli. "Instinct does not change."

"Instinct does not change," Eli muttered to himself as he turned from the window and headed to the other car. "You're right there! I should have followed my own fucking instinct and turned down this job."

Alpheus smiled. People. So messy. They lacked his clear mind. Before he brought about chaos, he wanted to see the sunset. He exited the car, strolled to the edge of the lot, and looked down on the Rosstown Plantation. The River Skweda, a silver talon, sliced through the heart of the three towns. As natural light left their world, the people rebelled with the artificial—bulbs. Alpheus sneered. He was always so unimpressed with the human species.

Rage against the dying of the light! Dylan Thomas wrote about failing to leave a mark on the world.

Alpheus nodded. He left a mark. These towns, these unimpressive humans in their artificial havens, they faced up to him. He would follow his instincts, take what he desired from Blue Falls, and leave them to rue their failings.

He smelled perfume and felt a hand trace down his arm. He didn't look at Autumn Lake. Didn't need to. She was trying to appeal to him sexually. "Can you be so certain that I, and not your husband, will fall if you initiate conflict?"

"What're you talking about, Birdman?"

"Refrain from using that term, Autumn. I'm talking about your smell and your touch. You are trying to appeal, yes?"

"Just a little bit of fun, *Alpheus*. Why are you always so serious?"

"Serious? You misunderstand. If I chose to have you now, I would. If your husband stepped from the car, I would kill him. They are merely actions. Behaviors, if you will. Seriousness is something you have constructed. Do you still want to play?"

She withdrew her hand. "I won't lie; you're interesting." She blew a bubble.

He didn't respond.

"You don't think I'm interesting?"

Alpheus watched several more lights burn into the night down in Rosstown. "Do not take it personally, Autumn. I don't find anyone that interesting."

"Goodnight, Alpheus." She took a few steps backward. "Maybe you should try to open your mind a little more—"

"Autumn?" It was Austin.

Alpheus didn't look back for the same reasons he hadn't even looked at Autumn yet; he simply didn't care.

"Just drinking in the views, lover."

"We're eating *now*."

"Coming. Bye-bye, Alpheus. See you tomorrow."

Alpheus turned his head so she could hear. "Tomorrow, you see Jake Pettman. Rest. Be ready. I will bring him to the summit where we will kill him. I cannot accept failure. That is not a warning or a threat. It is simply everything."

After he heard the car door close, he returned to his own car, started the engine, and descended the hill toward Blue Falls.

He didn't need a GPS. He'd spent an entire evening on Google Earth before the journey. It was part of his nature to know the territory. If he didn't know it as well as those he hunted, he would surely fail. So he drove all the way to Piper Goodwin's house, and there he parked.

Despite the protests of her subordinates, Louise, wielding weapon and torch, assisted the team in securing the area. It wasn't her style to just stand back and issue orders. Some of those at HQ in Maine considered it to be one of her failings. She considered it a strength. It showed sincerity in the decisions she made, and she believed it gave confidence to her officers that she wasn't just barking commands erratically.

Immediately, the dogs strained at their leads to get to the wooden hut at the back. Despite this, they opted to secure the log cabin first. It was a much bigger property, and so much more likely to carry a bigger threat within those walls. They left two officers with their guns trained on the hut just in case.

When it became apparent that no one would respond to their warnings, they aimed their torches and weapons at the cabin and moved in. They were prepared to break down the door, but it wasn't necessary; it was unlocked. They swivelled their torches in the darkness until they found the light switch. Not a soul was inside.

No one responded to the warnings at the wooden hut either. Gordon, Louise's most trusted officer from MSP, headed in first. "Door has been broken open." Holding his torch with his left hand, resting the gun on top of it with his right hand, he edged the door open with his foot. "Police!"

No response.

He entered and hit a light switch. "Clear! A strong smell of chemicals—" Ashen-faced, he stumbled out, leaned over, clutched his knees, and vomited.

Louise quickly moved to him. She put a hand on his shoulder and knelt in. "Gordon. Talk to me! Gordon?"

"Ma'am, I wouldn't go in there. Spare yourself."

She looked up. Other officers had already gone in. She heard other cries of anguish. She left Gordon and charged for the hut. She had to sidestep another officer exiting in a similar anguished state to Gordon. She smelled the chemicals before she reached the hut, so she covered her mouth and nose as she entered. "Don't touch *anything!*"

She didn't really need to give any warning about crime scene contamination. The two other officers in there weren't about to handle anything. They were too busy simply standing there, aghast.

Louise surveyed the smashed bottles, broken furniture, and the walls with the six trophies. Her first thought was, *Lifeless, yet so alive, as if screaming for help.* Dizzy with disgust and confusion, she stepped carefully to avoid smashed glass and slipping over loose chemicals. She then noticed two things that broke her.

The face on the farthest left was of a black person.

It was also small and could be that of a child.

A deep, guttural cry came from deep within. A cry which lasted during the moment in which she pounced forward, the seconds in which she drew her fingers over the pained leathery face, and the final flashes in which another officer was pulling her away. When she finally stopped, out of breath, she was sitting on the ground outside the hut. The dogs were barking again.

She heard Gordon's voice. "There's more. Round the back. The dogs have found more!"

TWO DAYS BEFORE JAKE PETTMAN LEAVES BLUE FALLS

Susannah was carving a red line into Kayla's face when Gabriel returned.

He raised the rifle that Susannah had left beside the open door of the bedroom. He winced as he did so, the burning in his wounded hand intensifying. "Move back!"

Susannah looked down at the mess she was making of Kayla's face.

"Move. Back. Now."

She laid the scalpel on the bedside table.

Gabriel watched the blood bubbling out the long gash on Kayla's beautiful face. He acknowledged the movement of her chest, concluding she was alive. "You didn't think I'd leave her, did you?"

"I did. Cowards don't come back."

"How did you know I wouldn't go to the police?"

She smiled. "You can't, can you, *Gabriel*?"

Gabriel took a deep breath.

"Yes, I know all about you. Kidnapper, murderer. Don't let this hobbling recluse lost in the woods fool you. I do maintain a connection with the real world, to do what needs to be done." She admired Kayla's face. "To get what I need." She stroked the undamaged side of Kayla's face. "Need compels us, doesn't it, Gabriel? It seems you may just love her after all."

"Take your damned hands off her and move back."

Suzannah lifted her hands free, showed her palms, and stepped backward.

"What have you given her?"

"Just something to keep her asleep."

"What the hell are you? Were you going to let her wake up after ... after ... what you do?"

"She would have passed, eventually. I just find that taking beauty following death affects the longevity of the flesh."

"No more. Seriously. *No more.* I don't want to hear it. This ends now, you twisted piece of shit."

Susannah smiled again. "A man of words or actions? Which is it, Gabriel?"

"I thought you'd read the news? We're going outside now, Susannah. We're going away from Kayla."

"Her knight in shining armor."

"Whatever has happened, whatever is to happen, I do have some humanity, Susannah. People like you don't have any."

"And there it is! A self-affirmation. The bad man with the moral compass. Ha!"

"You can die in here or outside. The choice is yours. I'd prefer to keep your diseased blood from Kayla."

"As would I." Susannah looked down again. "Such a beautiful face. Ah, very well, if killing me propels you from zero to hero, then lead the way."

"Killing you is just plain right. No other reason. Come. No hobbling either. None of that bullshit." He took several steps backward to clear the doorway, allowing himself enough space to get a fatal shot should she decide to turn for him. "Outside," he said when she drew level with the dining table.

"Do you ever think about the people you kill, Gabriel?" Susannah asked as they stepped outside.

"No. Do you?"

"Of course. All the time. I give them honor, immortality, grandeur—"

"Big words won't justify what you do."

"Is Kayla happy with her life?"

"Keep walking." He prodded the small of her back with the weapon, attempting to put more urgency in the psycho's step.

"You refuse to answer because you know the truth. She told me you killed her brother. You took her family from her. You destroyed part of her long before she came to me. But I'm offering her a chance to shine."

"Listen," Gabriel said as they reached the tree trunk base where Susannah had been chopping wood earlier. "Me and you are coming from very different places. You are a twisted fuck who kills children, whereas I'm someone on the edge who will do anything to survive and keep that girl alive in that room. Our paths didn't converge, so much as collide." Gabriel placed the rifle at his feet and pulled the axe from the wood where Susannah must have replaced it earlier. "You also cut off two of my fingers and forced me to look at your trophies in the hut. It's a miracle this conversation persists."

"So end it, then, Gabriel."

"Go to the back of your fucked-up hut."

"Why?"

"Because when Kayla wakes, I don't want her to see the mess I make of you."

Susannah shrugged and walked around the side of the hut.

"Are you not scared?" Gabriel asked, following her, the axe ready in his hand.

Susannah shook her head. "Not something I ever really had the pleasure of." Round the back of the hut, she turned to look at him and smiled. "And that's it, is it? You just —"

He swung, and the axe made a perfect arc through the air.

Thud.

"Put you down? I guess so, yes," Gabriel said, standing back and watching her slump against the rear of her evil hut. He'd managed to bury the axe quite deeply, and it had split her head to the center of her eyes.

Twitching, she slid to the ground. Her eyes still seemed to be focused on him, even though that clearly wasn't possible.

He spat on her. "Judge yourself before you start judging me."

Kayla woke while Gabriel tended to the wound on her face.

He'd managed to find some butterfly stitches and band-aids in Susannah's medical supplies and was sealing the wound as best he could. He'd also wrapped the stumps of his ruined fingers in a thick white bandage.

She was struggling to focus after being anesthetised, and her eyes rolled as she looked at him.

"Just rest," he said.

She said something, but her voice was hoarse, and he didn't quite understand.

He stroked her forehead, wet her dry lips with some water, and she went back to sleep.

In the afternoon, when she awoke again and the confusion had past, she remained lethargic and in a state of shock from her experience with Susannah.

When he said, "You don't have to worry; she's gone," she stared at him with bloodshot eyes and replied, "She said the same. That *you'd* gone. I felt safe again. It was a lie."

He felt his heart drop. "I've treated you badly. That

changes now. What *she* was, that's not what *I* am. I'm going to give you the life you deserve. I promise."

She didn't reply; instead, she turned her head from him on the pillow. She'd not even asked about her face. The pain must have been excruciating. She looked hollow.

He left some Tylenol on the bedside table and let her rest.

Later, after the sun had set, Gabriel took his third Adderall of the day. He was doing his best to space out the remaining doses to hold off withdrawal. He then managed to get the fire outside going. He warmed three cans of baked beans in the pot using the wooden tripod. He took her a bowl in with a spoon. "How're you feeling?" he asked from the door.

"It hurts," she said, crying.

He walked around the side of the bed and put the bowl of beans beside her. "I know how you feel." He held his bandaged hand in the air. "Never known a throbbing pain like it." He popped out two more Tylenol and handed them over with a glass of water. "I've been taking these three at a time."

She shook her head. "I'll get my own."

"If you wish. We will stay here another night; you really need the rest. Tomorrow, we will work our way through the tinned food in the kitchen, build our strength some more, and head off at night. There will be less chance of being seen, and it gives you more chance to stock up on sleep during the day."

"I don't understand. Where are we going? There's no way out. Don't you see that now?"

He shook his head. "I can't give up."

"It's over. Maybe they'll go easier on you if you turn yourself in now."

"Eat your beans, Kayla."

Later, Gabriel came into the room, holding a tatty paperback book. "I was going through one of her cabinets and look what I found." He showed her the cover: *Five Run Away Together* by Enid Blyton. "It reminded me of before. I think you enjoyed them."

At his house, while she'd been locked in his basement, he'd often read to her. One of those books had been *Five on a Treasure Island*. As much as she would never admit to it to him, she had listened, and he believed she'd found some enjoyment in the words.

"Would you like me to read to you?"

She turned from him and didn't respond.

He sat on the edge of the bed and began.

During the next day, between bouts of resting and eating, Gabriel read the entire book to Kayla.

She didn't respond, not a single time. But in the same way he'd persevered at his home, he persevered now too.

When he'd finished, he put the book on her bed next to a pile of clothes he'd found in one of Susannah's closets and pointed at them. "I think these will fit you. If you want to change, you can. You should also use her toothbrush in the bathroom. Ten minutes should be enough."

While he waited for her to change, Gabriel warmed a bowl of stew over the dying flame outside. Then he checked his belongings one last time. He'd found a backpack under the bed and had filled it with cans of beans and soups. He'd also packed some medical supplies, band-aids, antiseptic cream, and painkillers.

She came out of the bedroom wearing the same clothes.

It was her way of protesting, he decided. She wouldn't accept anything he offered—no enjoyment from his storytelling, no handful of painkillers, no clean clothes. While she was in the bathroom, Gabriel ran his hands through his hair. He'd slept badly last night and sighed. The incessant pain in his hand and his tapered withdrawal from Adderall were combining in harsh ways. He still had six uppers left, and it would be better to space them out as best he could.

He collected the stew from outside. The fire had died, but the embers were holding on for dear life. He considered going inside for a glass of water to kill them off good and proper but decided to let them suffocate instead. Inside, he spooned the stew into two bowls. He ate his quickly.

She came out the bathroom, and he pointed at her bowl. "Eat."

"I'm not hungry."

"We are walking to the Skweda. I don't know how long it will take us. It could be all night."

"That doesn't make me feel any hungrier."

Gabriel sighed. "You ready?"

"One more thing." She disappeared into the bedroom.

Gabriel slung the rifle over one shoulder. He patted the front of the backpack to double check the ammunition was in there. There were a couple of boathouses where the Skweda bent from Sharon's Edge to Blue Falls. This was his destination. To get what he wanted, he would have to be armed.

He threw the backpack over his other shoulder.

Kayla emerged from the bedroom, holding the book he'd just read to her.

"So, you did enjoy it?" he asked with a smile.

She marched to the front door and turned. "I'm taking it, because the first thing I'm going to do when I get away from you is read it to myself." She turned and exited.

Gabriel followed, sighing again.

14

ON THE DAY JAKE PETTMAN LEAVES BLUE
FALLS

I T WAS JUST past midnight when they took their first
break.

Jake sat on the mossy ground and watched the shafts of
light streaming through the tree canopy. Someone must
have been smiling on them from above. They couldn't have
moved at this pace without a full moon; the flashlight on his
cellphone would have been no substitute. He unscrewed
the top on a bottle of water they'd taken from the log cabin
and took several mouthfuls.

"Easy on that," Peter said, kneeling beside him to catch
his breath. "I don't know how long we'll be going at this for."

Jake rolled his eyes and screwed the top on the bottle.

"And I probably wouldn't sit down if I were you. Ants.
They can get quite big here."

"Worse things to worry about than an ant bite."

"*Bites* ... lots of them." Peter shrugged. "Just saying."

Jake grumbled and pulled himself into a kneeling position, like Peter. "Happy?"

"You *will* be now."

Jake munched on a salty cracker they'd also recovered from the log cabin. He nodded forward in the direction they were going. "Is this the right call?"

Peter sighed. "I don't know. What I do know is we're heading north, and eventually, we'll break out onto the banks of the Skweda."

"But then what? Do we even know he's heading there?"

Peter shrugged. "Sorry. The Skweda is all I can promise. It's too dark to track properly, not that I could at the pace we're going; we're practically jogging. But where else is he likely to go? The roads are blocked. The helicopters will be out in force come daylight I expect. The Skweda seems a very good option to me. Probably work his way onto the Connecticut River if he's bold enough!"

"Won't he need a boat?"

Peter shrugged again. "He's the chief of police. Well, *was*, I guess. He's resourceful, and he'll have a plan. There are boathouses along the Skweda, you know. Problem is, there are boathouses *both* ways. Unless we catch him up beforehand, we may be faced with a fifty/fifty before sunrise."

Jake stood and stretched. "Best get catching them up then."

Peter stood and coughed.

"Should have listened to me on those smokes."

Peter patted his chest. "Don't you worry about me. Years of scurrying through red-hot jungles has plated this respiratory system with iron."

"Good stuff. Lead the way, ironman."

Lillian knocked on Louise's door and poked in her head. "It's quarter past twelve, ma'am."

Louise stopped writing, put down her pen, and confirmed it with a look at her watch. "So it is, Officer Sanborn. You should head off."

"I'd like to stay, ma'am, if that's all right?"

"There's no point in missing your rest, Officer Sanborn. There's no move for us to make tonight. The dogs are tracking the scent through the forest, and if we don't get them by first light, the helicopters are on standby."

"Ma'am, that's not what I meant. I want to stay. With you."

"I don't follow."

"The shock you had, *before*, at the cabin. It must have been horrible."

Louise shook her head. "Listen. It was an irrational response. Just like the next person, I'm all for a good coincidence, but I know the chances of one of my daughters turning up at a log cabin during my own investigation are minuscule. You needn't worry, Officer Sanborn; clarity has been restored to my way of thinking."

"I don't buy that you're fine, ma'am."

"Excuse me, Officer?"

"With all due respect, you don't see something like that, *think* something you did, without experiencing a high degree of shock. I know I can't convince you to go home or even stop working, ma'am, but I would like to be here in case you need anyone to talk to."

Louise sighed and sat back in her chair. "How many times do you think I've been in shock since the day my family disappeared, Lillian?"

The first name again. The conversation had become a personal, rather than a professional, one.

Lillian forced back a gulp. "I can't imagine."

"A day doesn't go by that I don't wake up to the shock that they aren't here anymore. An hour doesn't go by that I don't shock myself into a stupor when my overactive imagination considers all the ways they may have died."

"I'm so sorry."

"Go home, Lillian, please. You are a good person. One of the best. But I can reassure you that your presence here is not needed this evening. I must cross the Ts and dot the Is in these notes for HQ. They're sending someone else for the Susannah Gott investigation. I've got too much on my plate with the current situation, and I don't want to diffuse my focus."

"Where did those victims come from?"

"Children? Yes, the medical examiner confirmed it. Sickening affair, it really is. We don't know where they're from. Her car has been located a couple of miles outside the woods, but it seems much too big of a task for her to pull off on her own. Susannah Gott has lived a recluse for the best part of fifteen years, but someone has helped her. It will be down to my colleague from Maine to find out if this is the case, and if so, who the mysterious person is." She rubbed her eyes. "Yes, I know. I sound invested. And yes, having seen what I saw today, *I am*. But we must stop Gabriel and get Kayla MacLeoid back first. We cannot deviate from this priority. Once we achieve this, I will offer our support to my colleagues with the Susannah Gott investigation."

"Okay, ma'am."

"Get some rest, Lillian. I'm confident that tomorrow—sorry, *today*—will be the day something finally gives."

―――――――

Alpheus checked his watch—2:14.

Many would say that Alpheus's decision to shun sleep and watch Piper's home all night was irrational and illogical; after all, where was she likely to go? However, Alpheus was not a man bound to logic and rationality but one bound to great instinct. He couldn't see *inside*, but he had her territory in his sights, and there it would stay until the sun rose, and he could swoop.

He reached into his glove compartment, past the plastic purple box which contained his beak, and plucked a pre-packaged sandwich with his sharpened claws.

Then, while he ate, he watched, affording his prey the respect she deserved.

―――――――

Kayla put her hand against the tree trunk and leaned her head into it. The book she'd vowed to hold onto slipped from her hands, and she slid to her knees.

A yard or so ahead, Gabriel said, "The Skweda. I can see it."

Kayla slumped to her side and heard the crunching of undergrowth.

"Kayla? Are you okay?"

Everything hurt—her arm, her face, her feet. *Everything.* She groaned. The sound and smell of his breath drew closer to her face. She tried to roll away from the monster who'd ruined her life but didn't get far. She was out of energy.

"Don't give up now. We're close, I promise."

"Leave me. *Please*, leave me." With her eyes closed, she

felt around the ground for the book. When her hand settled on it, she drew it toward herself.

"I *wouldn't* ever leave you. I could never leave you in this state."

She pulled the book to her chest. "You caused this." She closed her eyes. Fighting the maddening pain splitting her world in two, she searched for happier times. She put her arms around her toy monkey Morris, a present from a mother she'd been given precious little time with. She felt the touch of her brother Ayden as he took both her and Morris into his reassuring embrace. She felt herself being lifted into the air. "Ayden, swing me around. Swing me around like you used to!"

"I've got you. Just sleep, Kayla."

She felt weightless in her brother's arms. "Thank you, Ayden."

"It's me. *Gabriel*."

She opened her eyes and looked into her kidnapper's face. "Just leave me, please. Leave me to die."

"I got you, Kayla." Gabriel looked straight ahead as he carried her. "I got you."

She felt the first sunrays on her face as she clutched the book to her chest.

After dawn had finished decimating the murk in the woodland, Jake chanced a conversation with Peter, which he was certain would be rebuffed. "You never told me about the Vietnamese lady who engraved your lighter. Tong, I believe?"

Peter stopped leading the charge but didn't turn.

Yep, Jake, bad move. "Sorry, don't know what I was

thinking! Powerwalking all night in this heat and the constant fear of those ants biting me must have addled my brain."

"Why now?" Peter asked without turning. "Why ask me now?"

"Been a long trek, got me thinking how much time we've spent together—what we've been through together. Then I realized I hardly knew anything about you."

"Ditto."

"I hate that word, but it's a fair comment. Difference is you're a local legend, whereas I've got a lot to be ashamed of."

"You've probably got a lot to be proud of too." Peter sighed and turned. "Believe it or not, I was always planning on telling you about Tong, but you know, things got in the way."

"It hasn't been the quietest couple of months for sure. Sorry, I shouldn't have brought it up. Let's park it—"

"Better now than never. Tong was the only woman I ever loved. She deserves to be spoken about."

"Is she still alive?"

"No, but what does that have to do with love? Let's walk."

For the first time in hours, they walked side by side rather than in single file.

"I guess it's a rather predictable story. Young soldier gets stationed in a Vietnamese town and falls for a young farmgirl. I don't want to bore you with the details. I'm sure you can find something on Netflix that would cover the basics."

"I want to hear the basics. All of it. Anyone who captures your heart, old man, must be a special woman." He laughed. "Or at least patient!"

So, Peter told him his love story, and it was, as he'd suggested, a traditional one. A quick exchange of smiles on market day; her laughter as he attempted, badly, to introduce himself in Vietnamese; the free time he donated to supporting her with her farming responsibilities; the local cuisine he sampled around her family's dinner table.

"Looking different from the multitude of white American soldiers helped me in that regard! They liked to hear stories of my people's tragedy too. We shared a common bond in oppression, I guess. Tong's English was impressive, and she'd translate everything for her family. I grew close to them all ... even the brother."

"Even? Was he an older brother? Older brothers are *always* hard to win over."

Peter stopped, turned, and looked up at his tall companion. "He was working with the Vietcong, Jake. The sneaky little bastard was the enemy."

Thwap-thwap

"Jesus! Helicopters?" Jake said.

Peter nodded.

"Let's pick up the pace. Who knows what hell will descend if they find them before us."

PIPER'S FATHER—AT least Alpheus assumed he was her father—exited the house. He wheeled his golf bag to his Honda SUV, positioned it gently in the trunk—Alpheus always found it strange how much a man could love his golf clubs—then paused to look skyward, shielding his eyes. He nodded once, clearly happy with what the day was going to offer him, climbed into his vehicle, and drove away.

Ten minutes later, Piper's mother left the house. She

was dressed in a summery frock. Where she was going, he had no idea, nor did he really care. Maybe she was going to church; it was Sunday, after all.

Even though Alpheus had been prepared to kill *both* parents, he preferred this outcome. He only killed the elderly to put them out of their misery and likened it to swooping on a lame rabbit. Their deaths would have been for convenience.

Alpheus slipped his weapon into the holster under his jacket and exited his vehicle. There was no increase in body temperature or heart rate as he crossed the road. He didn't expect a fight. He knew Jake wasn't here, because the people who'd employed Alpheus had contacts within the police. He'd been reliably informed that Jake was currently gallivanting around the Rosstown plantation on a vigilante mission to save a kidnapped girl and put a corrupt chief to the sword. Alpheus had no doubt that what he was about to do would draw Jake out. No doubt at all. So, no need for adrenaline. Best saving that for later when things became more *confrontational*.

As he approached the Goodwin residence, he cast an eye over the two neighboring houses. It had only just dawned, so curtains were still closed. Of course, there was still a chance he may be spotted, but that contact within the police department would most certainly warn him and keep things at bay as best he could if the situation required it so.

He read the name of the house on the plaque by the door. *Misty Meadow House.* He wondered over the point of that and knocked on the door. He turned away from the door and slipped his P-19 from his holster. If Piper chanced a look through the spyhole, she wouldn't be able to see him screwing on the silencer.

There was no answer.

He tried several more times and was forced to accept the possibility the house may be unoccupied, that he had messed up. He'd never seen Piper *arrive* at the house; he'd just assumed she was there. He'd had it confirmed that she was still living here. He wondered if his lack of thoroughness would now cost him.

After a moment's thought, he decided his best option was to gain access to the house. He went around to the back where high fences would shield neighboring eyes from his actions. He peeled off his hooded top and used it to muffle the sounds of the smash when using a brick on the glass on the door. He reached in, unlocked the door, and entered.

He searched the entire house, quickly and efficiently, concluding, without any doubt, no one was present. Standing in the hallway, he had to admit the chaos of not knowing where Piper was had induced a moment of panic. He took a deep breath and holstered his weapon. Then he went to sit in the living room and think.

If she had been in the house overnight, she must have left earlier via the back door he'd just vandalised. He remembered seeing a gate at the end of the garden which could lead onto a back alley. He sat and waited, rooted to the spot, waiting for a moment of clarity. He watched the minutes tick by on a mantlepiece clock.

He started to formulate another plan, and when he was confident that it too could work, he stood. He noticed a woman on the front driveway.

He thought of the photo of the younger Piper in his possession. The resemblance was there.

He breathed a sigh of relief and slipped into the hallway to prepare for his catch.

15

WITH KAYLA ASLEEP in his arms, Gabriel approached James Trescott's boathouse. He rode a sudden surge of confidence, something he'd not had the pleasure of feeling since that moment they bypassed the roadblock in the van. However, considering how quickly everything had spiralled into shit the last time, he decided it best to temper his expectations right now.

The best thing about this whitewashed and crumbling boathouse, which jutted over the Skweda on its own platform, was that James was its single occupant. He knew this because his father, Earl, had been good friends with the old recluse. Gabriel recalled sitting on a small pier jutting from the platform, drinking Coca-Cola from a bottle, while the two men—ancient in his eight-year-old eyes—drank whiskey and laughed.

It must have been at least a mile to the next boathouse, so it would afford Gabriel the isolation and quiet he needed to take what he wanted by whatever means necessary.

As he got closer to the decaying structure, Gabriel was grateful to hear sounds within. It suggested James would be hard at work and not lounging about in his adjacent house, which would have put the old-timer into closer proximity to a phone and a weapon.

The boathouse was rimmed with unkempt grass and weeds, a good resting place for his ailing companion. The heat was beating down now, so Gabriel sought a large bush about midway down the structure which would at least provide Kayla with some shelter as she slept off the exhaustion which was, as she'd pointed out before, all *his* fault.

He stroked her pale face and kissed her forehead. He felt a tingle spread through his body—*not* that kind of tingle, a paternal kind. He wanted to believe that now his body and his perverse desires were responding to his cry for change.

As he rose and groaned over the state he was in. It wasn't just his damaged fingers, although they throbbed violently, or even the knife wound in his arm, which burnt like fire, but every *single* muscle in his body. He reached into his pocket for the medicine bottle, unscrewed it, and shook out the Adderall. Six left. He took one, sighed, wishing he could magically refill the bottle, and resealed the remaining five.

He cracked and straightened his back, filled his lungs with air, and gritted his teeth. *One last push, Gabriel. One last push. You owe it to her. She doesn't realize yet, but its only you who can give her the life she deserves.*

Thwap-thwap-thwap ...

A helicopter! He ducked beneath the bush with Kayla again and remained still. With his blood running cold, he watched the hulking monstrosity in the sky. It'd been expected, of course. In fact, it was surprising it'd taken this long. However, this didn't make it any easier to stomach. He took a deep breath. He just had to hope the pilot's attention remained *on* land and not the water. A long shot. The river wasn't exactly inundated with boats, but there were some, and just a few may allow him to blend in.

He waited for the helicopter to sweep back over the woodland he'd spent days in, then he was up and moving down the side of the boathouse, listening to the clanging sounds from within. He turned into the boathouse with his rifle at the ready. In contrast to its weathered and decaying exterior, the interior was orderly and clean. Four small boats were spaced out across the center. He noticed, immediately, two of them had motors, and his heart gave a leap of gratitude.

He spied James lying on a mechanic's creeper in his blue overalls. He was attending to damage on the underneath of one of the rowing boats; strangely enough, he was doing this by hammering, and Gabriel wondered what good that could really do.

"James," Gabriel said.

James stopped working.

"James, it's Gabriel Jewell."

James sat upright. He had long white hair pushed back in a ponytail and wore Coke-bottle glasses. He squinted. "Are you pointing a rifle at me, Gabriel?"

"Afraid so."

James held a finger in the air and looked to the right. "Did you hear that, son?"

"No, what was it?"

"The sound of your father turning in his grave."

The jab stung, simply because it was true. Earl would be horrified. Thank God, he wasn't alive to feel such shame, such *disappointment*.

"I don't have a choice, James. I'm all out of options."

"I'll give you a choice, young man." James rose to his feet. "Put down the rifle, and I won't kick your ass."

Gabriel smiled. "I can see why Dad loved you, but I really don't have enough time."

"What have you done to that poor girl?"

This *also* stung. "News travels fast. I've done nothing. *Nothing.* I don't expect you to understand, but it isn't like that. I care for her."

"No, I don't understand." He cracked his knuckles. "Tell me where she is, and I won't break you in two."

"She is safe, around the side of the house."

"Good."

He rolled up the sleeves on his overalls. "Now put down the rifle."

"Enough." Gabriel shook his head. "You're not going to fight me. I love your spirit, old man, but even if I was to lay down the rifle, you wouldn't stand a chance. I need a boat."

"Never much been in love with humanity, I admit that. And a bullet hole to the chest is not the way I pictured checking out. But if you think I'm giving you a boat to swan off with that poor girl—"

Gabriel fired the rifle in the air. Flecks of wood and paint rained down.

"That's my fucking roof."

"Let's start again, James. I need a boat, and *you're* going to help me."

Thwap-thwap-thwap.

"Because I'm out of time."

JAKE STARED AT the book in his hand. *Five Run Away Together*. The cover was spotted with blood. He felt his stomach tighten. "Do you think it's Kayla's?"

"I don't know," Peter said. "But it wouldn't be a bad thing. It would mean that east was the right choice."

Peter was referring to the moment they'd broken from the woodland onto the banks of the Skweda. On any other day, it would be impossible not to admire the water's blue glow beneath the sun on a cloudless day; on this day, they had to anxiously choose from east or west, knowing that Kayla's life depended on it.

A motorboat slid past them. Jake moved to the edge and was relieved to see a young woman was driving it.

Peter pointed in the distance. "The first boathouse is not too far."

"Nearer if we run."

Peter nodded, but his worn expression suggested his body didn't like the idea.

Thwap-thwap.

"Look." Jake pointed at a distant helicopter above the trees. "That'll be over us before we know it." He started to run toward the boathouse. "I want to finish this."

Peter ran alongside him.

As they drew closer to the hulking, white structure, they saw activity out front. "*Look!*"

"I see it." Peter sounded out of breath.

It quickly became clear that someone was wheeling a boat to the edge of the platform over the river. Peter suddenly stopped, out of breath, and knelt over, clutching his knees. "Take ... my ... rifle," he said between several lungsful of air. He let the strap slip from his shoulder, and the rifle tumbled to the ground.

"You all right?"

"Just ... *go!*"

Jake swooped for the rifle and continued the charge. Jake was not out of shape, but neither was he an Olympic sprinter. His legs ached. Sweat stung his eyes. He willed himself forward. *Come on, come on ...*

He thought of Kayla—innocent, broken and alone. *With no one to help her.*

He thought of Paul Conway—dead in his arms. *Because of him.*

He thought of Jotham, Mason, and all the other parasites. *Those who drain what little goodness exists in the world.*

And then he saw him.

The chief parasite.

Gabriel Jewell.

He was climbing into the boat he'd just pushed into the water.

Jake pushed harder. His lungs burned.

The motorboat's engine roared.

He's going to get away!

Thwap-thwap. The helicopter was closer now.

He waved one hand in the air as he stormed forward. "Here, here!"

Gabriel climbed out of the boat. A glimmer of hope!

Running so hard now, Jake felt as if he might vomit.

Thwap-thwap.

Yes. The helicopter was definitely getting louder. It was coming.

Gabriel returned to the boat, holding someone. It had to be Kayla. He climbed into the boat and laid her down. Then he straightened upright and just stood there.

Thwap-thwap-thwap-thwap. The noise of the blades intensified; the helicopter was surely landing.

Gabriel stood there, unmoving. *What was he doing?* It looked as if he was simply admiring the views of his river. Did he know he was finished? Had the incoming helicopter shattered his illusions of escape?

Jake stopped a few yards from the boat. His eyes burned from all the sweat, and his heart felt as if it would explode. He raised the rifle and trained it on Gabriel. Was he a good enough shot? He remembered Jotham's eyes just before he shot him. Nothing had steadied his trigger finger that day. *There was no place for men like these in this world. No place.* Still, he didn't trust his shot from this distance, and it may be best not to spook him when it was so close to being over.

Kayla was looking over the edge of the boat with a desperate hand waving in his direction. She was screaming something he couldn't hear over the deafening sounds of the helicopter blades.

He felt pulled toward her by her plea but forced himself to stay rooted. What was Gabriel's intention? Would he turn, would he be armed, would he shoot her? It was safer to keep his rifle trained on him. He chanced a look behind him.

The helicopter had touched down, and officers were exiting.

He saw Peter run toward him with a hand in the air, looking terrified. He wouldn't want Jake shooting Gabriel in the back, not now law enforcement were here to witness proceedings.

Don't worry, Jake wanted to shout, but knowing there was no point over the cacophony. *I won't. I want to, so bad, but I won't.*

He turned back to see Gabriel pointing his rifle at him. *Shit*— Jake heard the gunshot but felt nothing.

A second gunshot sounded. Gabriel tumbled backward into the Skweda.

Jake spun back.

An officer was kneeling a yard or so from the helicopter, aiming his rifle.

JAKE IGNORED THE commotion building around him while he marched to the platform's edge and stepped over the chain mooring the boat. It swayed under his heaviness, but he kept his footing as he scooped up Kayla. When he saw the bloodstained bandages on her face and arm, he felt his heart sinking.

The helicopter ceased its racket, and some dogs started up instead. In the distance, he could see canines emerging from the woods and leading more officers this way. The crime scene was about to get overstaffed.

Despite his tired legs, he managed to get Kayla out of the boat, and he sat on the platform. He glimpsed at the water, half-expecting to see Gabriel rise from the murky depths, ready for one last throw of the dice, but the water remained still.

He looked at Kayla's face. She was awake but didn't speak. She seemed to be in a state of shock or exhaustion. Probably both. He smiled at her, stroked her hair from her face, and thought of Paul Conway. "You're safe now."

And I'm glad.

So very glad.

16

LOUISE thrust her head into the interview room where Jake was signing his statement. He'd spent a few hours on it since the helicopter had returned him and Peter to town. Having reread it several times, he was confident he wasn't incriminating himself in any way. Much to the dissatisfaction of this stony-faced visitor, he was sure.

Jake couldn't help himself. "It all worked out in the end."

Louise snorted. "There are so many ways we can take you downtown over the way you've conducted yourself."

Jake shrugged.

"From what I hear, we saved your life in the end," she said.

"The bastard missed. Your officer just got the shot off before me."

"Strange how Gabriel missed though, don't you think?"

Jake had been thinking the same thing but didn't grace it with a reply.

"A sharp-shooting chief of police, by all accounts.

Maybe he saw something he liked in you. The lawless approach, perhaps?"

Jake glared at her. "Believe me, there was nothing Gabriel Jewell liked in me. And the feeling was mutual. I'd be the last person you'd see at his funeral."

"For a funeral, we need a body."

"I'm sure you'll drag it up. Although, I'd suggest leaving him to rot in the dirt at the bottom of the river. How's Kayla?"

"She's resting in the hospital. Stitched up. It's a miracle she didn't end up with blood poisoning." Louise turned to go. "This conversation has gone on long enough. Bye, Mr. Pettman."

"Lieutenant?"

Louise turned back. "Did you not hear me?"

"The log cabin. Those faces. What was that? Who did that?"

Louise shook her head, smirked, looked down, and clucked her tongue. "Do you know what the best thing you could do right now is, Mr. Pettman?"

Jake shrugged.

She looked back up. "Leave. *Leave* Blue Falls. You are a dangerous man. It's a wonder people around you haven't started dying. If you stay, it'll only be a matter of time." She turned and left the room before Jake could muster a sarcastic response.

A young male officer who had clearly attempted, badly, to thin out his eyebrows showed Jake and Peter to the door. As he escorted them out, he wore a stern expression, but Jake struggled to take a man with such patchy eyebrows seriously.

As they descended the steps, Jake asked Peter, "I hope your reception wasn't as ice cold as mine."

"Did you get coffee and a sandwich?"

Jake shook his head.

"No, then I guess it wasn't."

"Bloody hell. Am I really public enemy number one?"

"Not in my opinion, but with Jotham and Gabriel out of the picture, stands to reason they will now look elsewhere."

"Great. Did you see Lillian in there?"

"No, why?"

"Just wanted to see how she was getting on. Hopefully better than the lieutenant; she looked frayed."

Peter smiled. "I think you'll get a surprise when you look in the mirror."

"Thanks. You don't look too bad, considering."

"Not much to influence, really. I was already *weathered* long before tonight."

"How'll you get your pickup from the woods?"

Peter checked his watch. "It's only midday, so I'll shower first. I've then got a favor I can call in."

"I could take you if you want."

"You're okay! No offense, Jake, but a short break from you will do me the world of good!"

"See, public enemy number one!"

Peter put his hand on his shoulder. "Hey, you know I really love you."

After they went their separate ways, Jake walked to his car that he kept on the side street which ran behind the Goodwin property. He eyed up the back gate into the garden. He'd already sent three texts from the station, none of which had been returned, and was desperate to see her. A hot shower wouldn't go amiss either.

However, Louise's harsh words at the station were playing on his mind, and Piper didn't deserve his edgy mood. He wondered if a drive might settle him first.

He hopped in his Ford and drove past the Blue Falls Taps and considered the Holbrooks; would they appreciate his condolences? Probably not. What had happened to Molly was far from his fault, but still his existence, as another living Bickford, would only serve to remind them of what had eventually caused their greatest tragedy—their diseased heritage. So, he gave that a miss.

He considered another watering hole outside of town though. A couple of beers may just take the edge off, but a quick glance in the rearview mirror at his dishevelled appearance convinced him to spare the afternoon drinkers an eyesore. Noticing also that he didn't smell the best, he cracked the window to bring fresh air into the equation.

Struggling to make a firm decision on where to go, he found himself edging toward Lookout Corner. After parking there, exiting and heading to the raised platform to stare out over the rock that was synonymous with the town and appeared on both the population sign and every available postcard, he wondered what had drawn him back here again.

"You are a dangerous man. It's a wonder people around you haven't started dying. If you stay, it'll only be a matter of time."

She was right, of course. It had been the same in Salisbury, and it was the same now, here in Blue Falls. Trouble had a way of finding him. Of that there was no doubt. And although he found resolution in the desperate situations he became embroiled in, there was *always* collateral damage.

He thought of the people he'd grown close to in Blue Falls: Piper, Lillian, Peter ...

"Leave. Leave Blue Falls."

He sighed and turned toward the undergrowth where, many years previous, they had discovered the innocent children. "I'm sorry for what my ancestors did to you. There is good in Blue Falls. There really is. Now, without Jotham MacLeoid, Mason Rogers, and Gabriel Jewell, this place can be what it deserves to be. Kayla MacLeoid can be who she wants to be."

"Leave. Leave Blue Falls."

Jake sighed and watched the blue water cascading over the rock. "I will, Lieutenant. I will."

Peter looked up at the shower head, hit the start button, and the hot water streamed onto his weathered face. He wasn't sure if he was a quick shower kind of guy or just an impatient bastard; however, today he made an exception and dragged out the process. The dirt and sweat on his body had formed a second layer of skin.

After his shower, he kicked his dirty clothes in the direction of the hamper, opting to make the decision of whether to wash them or just burn them after a well-earned breakfast of corned beef hash and a pair of eggs, sunny-side-up. And one last smoke. It would be the final instalment in his process of destressing. After that, things would change: no more greasy breakfasts, no more smoking and—he smiled —no more following Jake Pettman half-cocked off on his vigilante missions. He was getting too old for this shit.

His way of helping would now be exclusive to the Abenaki Council. So many of his people were in need of help in the Rosstown plantation. He recalled Felicity Davis and her two children—innocents embroiled in a violent shitstorm which had ultimately cost them their lives. Case in point. He should have done more there.

After fastening his bathrobe, he opened the bathroom door, expecting his new housemate, Mason, to come bounding in to add a sparkling layer of dog saliva to his freshly scrubbed legs.

No such luck.

It was also odd because Mason had become his shadow since taking up residency here.

"Mason?" He paused, expecting to hear those little legs pounding stairs.

Nothing.

He approached the banister and leaned over. "Mason?" Again, he waited for the sound of scurrying.

Again, nothing.

Had he left the back door ajar? Had he left poor Mason to the mercy of traffic? Concern bubbled in his stomach as he descended the stairs. His calves also burned; the last couple of days weren't sitting right with a man of his years.

Midway down the stairs, he heard barking. He welcomed the relief, although, for the life of him, he couldn't remember shutting his little man up in the living room. It seemed his muscles weren't the only thing suffering with age; his brain cells were too.

Mason scratched at the door and yapped some more.

"Coming, fella!" He opened the door, slipped to his knees, and let Mason find his face with his tongue. "Easy, boy!"

After the warm embrace, he let Mason scurry into the

185

room and felt his cellphone buzz in his pocket. As he entered the living room, he removed his phone and read the message. It was from Jake: *Stay off the smokes*. He smiled and looked up. His breath caught in his throat.

A large man was sitting on his sofa, holding Mason in the crook of one arm and stroking his small head. In his other hand, he held a silencer pistol.

Peter eyed his open living room door, which he could have a crack at diving through before the intruder got a shot off. But Mason? *Shit!*

"I don't dislike dogs, Peter. Listen. I have no business here with your animal. There's no need for him to be harmed." He pointed at the single chair opposite him with his weapon. "My business is with you. Only. Sit. Please."

Peter looked at Mason. *You stupid dog. You should have warned me!*

Mason tried to pull away from the intruder to get to his owner.

The bastard held him back.

Mason yelped.

"Don't worry, boy. I'm staying right here." Peter sat on the chair. "My old man once said to me that every Abenaki was living on borrowed time. That, eventually, the white devil would always come to your door. I kind of hoped things had moved on enough to stop that happening. Seems I was wrong."

The man smiled. "I am sorry to disappoint you. I am not the white devil."

"I see. Just another white man here to cause harm."

"I am more than just another white man. My name is Alpheus Bird. And a friend of yours has brought me to your door this evening."

Peter couldn't help chortling. "A British friend, by any chance?"

Alpheus smiled. "Maybe, then instead of blaming the white man, you should be blaming your choice of friends?"

"Listen, Alpheus. I can see you hold yourself in high regard, but devil or more than human, it matters not to me. I spent a chunk of my life in Vietnam alongside good men, and I can categorically say there are few, if any, better than Jake. If I must die for someone, then, by Christ, let it be him."

"Noble words."

"I don't care what you think of my words, but I'll remain polite so I can ask two things of you. One, you let Mason go. He's a puppy. And two, you let me smoke. I promised myself one last smoke today. I think I deserve to keep that promise to myself."

"My own father fought in Vietnam. His life was saved on more than one occasion by men, I would imagine, such as yourself." Alpheus released Mason. "So, for that, I will grant both your requests, but I cannot change the outcome of this encounter, so I'd prefer it if you didn't ask that of me. I am not a man who feels guilt, but I am a man who appreciates. I would like you to have my appreciation for your sacrifices in war."

Mason scurried onto Peter's lap.

Peter kissed the dog's head.

"You love dogs?" Alpheus asked.

"More than any living human."

"I prefer animals too."

Peter reached for the packet of cigarettes on the table beside him, opened it, and placed one in his mouth.

"I like the way they get what they want. They're driven

only by instinct and desire. Humans are too cluttered," Alpheus said.

Peter noticed his hands were shaking as he raised the Zippo and lit his cigarette. His eyes fell to the engraved name. *Tong*. It offered him a moment of inner peace. He took a deep drag, closed his eyes, and exhaled it with a sigh. When he opened his eyes, he said, "I agree. We are. *Cluttered.*"

Alpheus nodded. "In another life, we may have been friends, Peter. However, in this life, I have chosen to have none."

"That sounds sad," Peter said and took another puff.

"On the contrary, it makes everything *clear.*"

"Never been in love, Alpheus?"

Alpheus slowly moved his head from side to side.

"That's a shame."

Alpheus shrugged. "Tell me how your last adventure in love ended, Peter."

Peter snorted. "Good point." He took another drag and blew it out with the words. "But I don't think I could tell you this story before the end of the smoke, Alpheus."

"Well, maybe you should try. After all, if it's true what men such as yourself often say, that it is your greatest loves which define you, then this tale deserves to be told one last time."

"It begins with a girl. Beautiful inside and out."

"I hear it often does."

"Her name was Tong, and she was the only one—and I mean this, Alpheus—*the only one* who ever made me feel that way."

Alpheus nodded. "That's nice. I cannot imagine those feelings, but I'm glad you enjoyed them."

"I did, every second, until ..." He paused to smoke greedily.

"Until tragedy?

Peter nodded.

"It seems all the greatest loves end in such a way."

Peter noticed he was over half-way through his cigarette. "Maybe I should just finish this and let those sleeping dogs lie."

"For me, you can, but I am listening, Peter. I am offering that to you. I'm a captive audience."

Mason licked Peter's chin.

Peter pushed him down. "Easy, boy. The story is short but by no means sweet. I caught the brother making homemade bombs. He was working with the Vietcong."

Alpheus raised his eyebrows. "The sworn enemy."

Peter nodded while he smoked.

"Cluttered, you see, Peter. A manmade creation. A war is not natural behavior. What happened?"

Peter felt a tear in the corner of one eye. He had two, potentially three drags left on his cigarette. And then what? Oblivion? He regarded the strong man, so assured, so *natural* in the way he wielded that weapon, preparing to kill. Peter was all out of options. He took another drag, then looked at the cigarette. He had been wrong; there was only one puff left ... if that.

"I told my superiors," Peter said. "They stormed the farmhouse."

"Your mistake perhaps?"

Peter nodded. "It was loyal behavior, but yes, a mistake."

"They didn't let you go with them, did they?"

"No, they didn't. In fact, they had to restrain me." He looked at his cigarette. "Almost done."

"Finish the story."

"The story ended, Alpheus, without me there. Everyone in the house died that day. The son may have been Vietcong, but the family weren't prepared to give him up without a fight."

"More clutter."

"Always." Peter finished his cigarette and put it out in the ashtray. He gulped when he saw Alpheus readying his weapon. "I warn you," Peter said with a smile. "They say I have nine lives."

"How many have you used?"

"I never counted."

"I will give you the certainty you deserve. This will be your last one. It will also be painless. The velocity at which this bullet enters your head will render you unconscious before the damage."

"You make it sound pleasant," Peter said, his stomach turning. "Just one more thing, before?"

"Of course."

"No one else needs to die, do they?"

"Rest now, Peter. It is no longer your concern."

Peter fell into blackness.

Using a tissue, Alpheus soaked up some of the blood from around the black hole in Peter's forehead. He glanced at the pulpy grey matter which plastered the walls. It didn't disgust him in any way; however, it would have the desired effect on the individual this was being staged for.

Peter's eyes remained wide open, which would make Alpheus's next move even easier.

He held Peter's cellphone in front of the dead man's

face. The facial recognition system sent Alpheus straight through to where Peter had been last: a message from Jake Pettman.

His reply didn't need to be detailed. Two simple words would have the desired effect. The bond between the two men had been strong.

Help me.

Then Alpheus copied Jake's phone number into his own cellphone. He placed the phone on the table beside the ashtray, which contained Peter's final stubbed cigarette, stroked the puppy's head, nodded a farewell to the dead man, and departed.

Help me.

He called Peter's cellphone. It seemed to ring endlessly. When it finally offered a teasing click and a hiss of static, he felt a rush of hope, before groaning over the sound of Peter's recorded message.

He drove in a way he hated but was becoming ever more regular these days: recklessly.

When he arrived at the door of Peter's house, he found it ajar, and as he pushed it open, he said, "Please, God," over and over, trying to ignore the fact he'd never been a religious man, and if there was a God, Jake owed him a serious slap in the face for all his years of questionable behavior.

Mason ran to his feet, lifted himself, and gripped onto his shin.

Something was wrong.

"Peter?"

No reply.

Even as he turned into the lounge, his insides cold but

his skin burning hot, he half-suspected what he would see. Experience had taught him well. *Bitterly* well.

Peter stared straight ahead. A line of blood trailed over his nose from the hole in his forehead.

"Why?" Jake asked. He paused, part of him somehow hoping one of his closest friends would somehow shrug this off as an insignificance and reply. He scanned the mess on the wall. He went to his friend and knelt. He used his thumb and forefinger to close the old man's eyes. His hand settled on his good friend's Zippo. He read the name again. *Tong*.

And then he threw back his head and raged at God for that serious slap in the face he'd just delivered.

17

UNABLE TO FULLY comprehend what he'd just seen, Jake stumbled from the house and steadied himself against the porch railing.

He caught a glimpse of a large brown-gray squirrel scurrying up one of the trees on the road opposite the house. He followed its path until only its orangey-brown underside was visible from way up high, then it was gone. It was a creature so adept at disappearing, at evading its predators.

Jake, on the other hand, was anything but. There was no escape for prey like him. Three thousand miles from home. A town in the middle of nowhere. And still, he'd been found.

He threw up over the side of the railing. Wiping his mouth with his sleeve, he turned to look at the open door of the house. Then, he fully acknowledged what he'd just seen inside that room.

Death.

And the inescapable conclusion that no matter where he, Jake Pettman, went, death would surely follow, and everything he loved would be lost.

His cellphone beeped. The message came from a number not stored in his directory: *I hunt from way up high.*

With hands still trembling from the discovery in the living room, he tried desperately to reply to quiz the sender about his identity, but he didn't get far before the next message came through: *The world looks up to me. You look up to me.*

Jake shook the cellphone. "Fuck off! Who're you? What do you want from me?"

Beep. *Ross Hill. Through the Broken Rocks and to the edge. Come, Jake, and look up to me.*

Jake felt the corners of his mouth twitching as he thought, *Is this the person? The person responsible for that abomination in this house?* The likelihood of this being the killer sent a burst of adrenaline through Jake, which steadied his shaking hand. He managed to rattle off his reply, *Why don't you come and hunt here, prick? We can discuss what you've done.*

He paced the porch, waiting for the reply.

Beep. *I hunt where I please. This world is mine. I do not argue for what is my right. Twenty-five minutes, Jake. Not a second more.*

Jake clenched his teeth as he punched in his reply. *Fuck you. My terms. I'm standing where you left your last mess.* He stared at the screen, waiting for the murderous bastard to consent. No reply came, so Jake took that as a sign that the prick had accepted his counter invitation. He leaned against the railing again and tried to sight the evasive squirrel. He didn't but spoke out loud to the animal anyway. "The difference between us is I'm done running."

His cellphone beeped. He opened a photograph. He pulled so hard on the railing with his single hand that he heard it splinter. The photograph showed Piper Goodwin slumped in her wheelchair. Her head hung forward, and her dark hair streamed over her face and into her lap.

Jake took his hand from the railing before he broke it.

She was perched at a cliff edge.

His cellphone beeped. *My little eyas. It is almost time to take her from her nest so she can fly too. Twenty-four minutes now, Jake. Not a second more.*

JAKE'S SPEEDOMETER RACED past ninety as he cleared the crossroads.

The driver of one vehicle screeched to a halt, while the driver of another possessed the sound reflexes to screech around Jake's Ford.

Jake had no time to reflect on how lucky he was to survive—neither did a moment exist for him to ponder the chances of him facing one of his worst fears again less than a week after the last time. High-speed driving wasn't for everyone. It certainly wasn't for Jake Pettman.

There was no time because, in this moment, existed an even greater fear for Jake. The death of someone *close* to him. The death of someone *because* of him.

With his horn, he warned several vehicles that he was about to attempt the unthinkable, swung to the other side of the road, and cleared them.

Their expressions as he passed were a mix of disgust and disbelief.

He was thankful that no vehicle intercepted him on the wrong side of the road—not because of his own survival but because the survival of another depended on his imminent arrival at Ross Hill.

As he cleared the rotary in which he'd almost killed an

unseated biker days before, Jake checked his cellphone hoisted on the windshield. ETA was 13:12, but that was calculated at the speed limit he was currently ignoring, so hopefully, he'd buy himself more time.

He looked at the clock on the dash—13:02. He had sixteen minutes until ... until ...

Someone close to him died because of what he once was.

He pushed his speedometer to a hundred as he approached the bridge that cut over the Skweda into Sharon's Edge.

Déjà vu.

Five days earlier, he'd hit this bridge at a similar speed. He'd drawn so close to the bumper of Chief Gabriel Jewell's Audi that he could taste his exhaust fumes. Gabriel was a cold-blooded killer who needed shutting down, but ...

Kayla MacLeoid, a fourteen-year-old girl, had been locked in his trunk.

Jake had abandoned the chase after the phone call which informed him of this. But not this time. This was one journey Jake wouldn't abandon. *Couldn't abandon.* He turned off the bridge and negotiated several roads at breakneck speed. Eventually, he turned onto a highway that speared into a rural area of cornfields.

In this direction, the sunlight intensified. He slammed down the sun visor. It didn't help. He squinted and kept his foot down. Another glance at his cell now showed his ETA to be 13:11. He'd bought himself an extra minute.

He checked the clock again—13:08.

Close. In fact, he could see the hill looming ahead on the right. The turnoff was close. He knew what he was looking for. A yard-high rock wearing the painted words: *The Summit of Ross Hill.* It was time to start slowing for the sudden turn—

A loud boom made him flinch. The car jerked to the right. The taste of bile made him wince. His death was close ... *her* death was close. He'd never experienced a blowout, and every single nerve ending burned as he lived his worst nightmare, but he desperately held onto the words of advice his best friend, Michael Yorke, had once given him. *"Grip that steering wheel like your life depends on it, because it does. And avoid the brakes. Hit them and you'll spin. Let the car slow gradually."*

The pull on the car was like nothing Jake had ever experienced. He stared out the window over his glowing white knuckles as the car was sucked back and forth from a straight path. He let the car slow naturally, but it wasn't happening fast enough. Then the car felt as if it was being yanked. He saw the yard-high stone that pointed to the summit of Ross Hill racing to meet him head on.

BLOOD RAN INTO Jake Pettman's eyes. He leaned on his rented Ford's hood—it was that or go arse over tit—and surveyed the bent fender.

A deep voice behind him asked, "You okay?"

He held up the back of his hand to signal he was, then felt the hand on his shoulder; the Samaritan had not bought his bullshit. Feeling some steadiness return, Jake abandoned his smoking hood and stood upright, forcing the man's hand to fall away. "I need your help."

Jake's Samaritan was seventy-plus, but his tense and eager pose suggested he would be as effective as a man half his age. *Good. Time is running out.*

Jake used his sleeve to rub blood from his eyes. "What's the time, *exactly?*"

"Eighteen minutes past one."

Fuck. Jake slammed a fist on his crumpled hood. *Fuck ... fuck ...* "I'm out of time." He eyed his vehicle. *Bastard car.* The crash must have put him under for almost ten minutes. He regarded the elderly man again and shielded his eyes. The summer sun was coming in strong. Jake spied the old red Buick the man had arrived in. The door was open, and the engine was still running. "I need you to take me to the top of Ross Hill."

"If I take you anywhere, son, I'm taking you to the hospital."

"That's not an option."

"It's the only option. You're at death's door—"

Jake stepped forward.

The old man recoiled but struck a pugnacious pose. "You're not thinking clearly, son."

You got that right. Which is why I'm not brushing you aside. Jake looked at the Buick again. *I don't think I could aim that beast straight right now.* Jake scanned an empty highway framed by cornfields. "I'm not the bad guy here. You need to take me up there." He pointed to the summit of Ross Hill. "Before anybody dies." He nodded at the Buick. "I don't think me and your old girl are going to get on all that well, but I'll give it a whirl if I have to."

The old man sighed. "Well then, I'm driving. She's the only family I got."

Fighting back a wave of nausea, Jake said, "We need to leave right now."

The old man nodded. "Get in, then, but you better be the good guy."

Jake only stumbled once as he approached the Buick. He was optimistic that control was finding its way back to him. Jesus, he hoped so. God only knows what awaited him at the top of Ross Hill. Jake opted for the back seat, believing he would remain more threatening than riding shotgun.

The elderly man passed an oil-stained rag to him. "Sorry, it's all I have." He patted the wheel. "But it serves my baby well when she's bleeding."

"It'll serve me well too, thanks." Jake pressed it to his leaking forehead. "But we have to hurry."

The old man responded and exited the highway onto the dirt path up Ross Hill. "What are we going to find up there?"

Jake felt his nausea build but took it as a good sign that his adrenaline was ramping up. "You mean, what will *I* find, old man. You'll be staying well back."

"It sounds like you're going to war."

"If I'm too late, you can bet I will be."

His cellphone beeped. He cast the rag aside, slipped the cell from his pocket, and read the message: *I warned you.* The cell beeped again. Jake opened the photograph with a trembling finger. The phone slipped from his hand. He took a deep breath, desperately trying to process what he had just seen. He clenched his hands, focused on the roof of the car, then roared. At the same time, he punched the back of the passenger seat again ... and again.

"War it is then," the old man said.

———

The old man parked by two other cars.

"Please stay here," Jake said, opening the door.

"I would, son, but you still need to give me some indication of why."

Jake looked over the seat at him. "Innocent people are dying."

"We need the police then."

"Police around here are good for nothing. Have you never noticed that?"

The old man nodded. "You have a point there, but it's all we have."

"Listen, give me twenty minutes. If I'm not back, call them."

The old man sighed. "You *are* definitely the good guy?"

"In a fashion."

"Okay, well here's my counter offer then. I'm coming with you."

Jake shook his head. This old man reminded him of Peter, and he felt loss burning inside. "No. I won't put anyone else in danger. Whatever this is, I must finish it. *Alone.* I need a weapon. Can you help me?"

The old man thought for a moment and shrugged. "There's a tire iron in the back."

"That'll do." Jake went to the trunk, popped it, and reached in for the heavy metal bar which sat beside a jerrycan. He held it up and stared at the folded lug nut wrench at the end. Peter's remains had been testimony to the fact that whoever had brought him here was armed with a gun. It was unlikely he'd get close enough to use a tire iron.

He recalled the photograph of Piper's empty wheelchair lying on its side by the cliff. If it was real, if this monster had tipped her over the edge, then—he bounced the tire iron from one hand to the other—it would take more than bullets to stop him.

He closed the trunk. It echoed through the silence of Ross Hill.

The old man came alongside him. "You should let me come."

Jake shook his head. "There's enough blood on my hands. Just wait for me to come back; twenty minutes is all I ask."

The old man sighed.

"And one more thing. If someone else comes back other than me, then drive. Drive as fast as you fucking can. And don't look back."

"Uh-huh."

Jake turned and marched toward the entrance to the hill's summit with the images of both Peter dead in his chair and the overturned wheelchair burning in his skull. He threw the tire iron from one hand to the other, gritting his teeth.

A gunshot shattered the silence of Ross Hill.

Jake swung, his tire iron ready, and saw the old man leaning against the open door of his vehicle, clutching his neck.

Standing by the adjacent car was a tall black man aiming a gun. *An ambush.*

"*No!*" Jake charged.

He was too late. The man who'd been hiding in the adjacent car put one more bullet in the good Samaritan, watched him tumble, and turned the weapon on Jake. "I'd stop if I were you, big boy."

Jake didn't. His adrenaline was too high. The man didn't fire. Jake kneeled beside the old man. The vehicle would now act as a shield between him and the gunman. He looked down at the old man; he didn't need to take a pulse to know he was gone. His neck was ruined, and the second shot had gone through his eye.

Rage burned inside Jake. He gripped the open car door.

The urge to hop in, kickstart the engine, and mow down the prick was intense. He'd have a bullet in the head even before his arse touched the seat.

"Step out, big boy."

Jake leaned over and looked under the old man's vehicle. He saw the gunman's feet *still* by his own car. "How about you step round here?"

The man laughed. "How do I know you aren't packing?"

"You don't."

"Although I'm guessing not; otherwise, you'd have fired on me, wouldn't you?"

"Kind of wondering why you didn't fire on me, actually. Maybe you're a crap shot?"

The man laughed again. "Nothing crap in this shooting, big boy." Jake heard him spit on the ground. "Just got instructions to take you around alive. A shame. I fancied it myself, but money talks. Shit, whoever you pissed off wants you dead bad. This'll set us up for life."

Us. There were more. "Where's Piper?"

"On the summit, where I've been told to take you."

"I can take myself, thank you."

"I'll make sure, if that's okay."

Jake watched the prick's feet travel around the front of the old man's vehicle. Jake propped the tire iron, handle side up, against the front left wheel, and started to rise. "Did you kill my friend?"

"Can't claim credit for that, I'm afraid."

By the time Jake was at full stretch, the killer was a yard in front of him, training his gun on his head.

"Hands where I can see them."

Jake obliged.

"Now, peel off the jacket and give me a twirl."

202

Jake removed his jacket, held it in his hand, and turned. "Happy?"

"Always happy."

Jake smiled. "You want me to take off my jeans too?"

The man laughed. "You ain't hiding anything in jeans that tight."

"You sure? You don't want to pat me down? Are you worried you might get a little thrill when you see what I'm carrying?"

"You got a big mouth. Shame it's not me who gets to shut it up."

"Can I put my jacket back on now?"

"By all means, and then we head that way."

The stupid bastard pointed toward the summit, so Jake seized his opportunity. He swung his jacket and blanketed the gun. The killer fired, but at that point, he was off target. Jake's hand darted for the upright tire iron at the wheel and swung upward so it connected with the gunman's chin.

His head jerked backward.

Jake pounced, slamming the tire iron into the killer's ribs.

He doubled over, allowing Jake to sidestep and drive the metal tool into his spine. *Crack.* The gunman stumbled, tripped over the old man's body, and fell.

Jake grabbed the bastard's hair. He dragged him to look down at his victim. "Look at him! I want you to take that with you!" Jake yanked again and dropped the killer's head onto the edge of the driver's seat, then slammed the door.

Thump

And again.

Thump

And again and again and again.

Crunch ... crunch ... crunch

203

He slammed until he was out of breath and staggered backward.

The body slipped free and crumpled onto the corpse of the old man.

He turned away in disgust at the sight of the killer's pulped head, then swooped for the gun. He turned and marched toward the entrance. He looked from the tire iron in one hand to the black stainless-steel firearm in the other. Jake had never been here before, but he was reassured by the signpost for both *The Summit* and *The Broken Rocks.* He approached a gate, lifted the latch, and went through it.

He started on a narrow dirt path that wound through a small patch of trees. Ahead, where the trees ended, he could see several mounds of broken rocks at the foot of a grassy field which sloped upwards.

He recalled the message on his phone: *Through the Broken Rocks and to the edge. Come, Jake, and look up to me.*

They'd picked a location where stealth wasn't a great option, and even attempting any would be a waste of valuable time. So he quickened his pace, weaving around indents in the uneven surface, feeling his heart and breathing up-tempo—

Sudden pressure in the side of his left thigh just above his knee sent his legs crashing together. As he fell, he kept a firm grip on his weapons with his arms extended. A mistake. His chin hit the ground, and a vibration rocketed through his skull. Everything flashed.

Something slammed onto Jake's hand.

He cried out, snapping his hand away, leaving his gun unattended in the dirt.

A hand swooped down, and the gun was thrown hard into the undergrowth.

Jake released the tire iron with his left hand and reached for the foot. It was a useless endeavor, and the assailant's foot snapped back and kicked him hard in the side of the face. The world turned momentarily white again, but he found it in himself to roll with the blow to try to minimize the damage. When his vison cleared, he saw the upside-down face of his female assailant, leaning over him so her two pigtails hung down. She had teardrops tattooed onto her young face.

"The bigger they are," she said, "the harder they die." She blew a bubble and backed away.

Jake's head flopped to one side. He spat out blood. "We all die."

"And you, today," she said, pacing around him.

She'd inflicted considerable pain on him; he wanted so desperately to get hold of her. He threw out his left hand, but she was careful enough to leave a suitable distance as she circled. "Is she alive? Is Piper alive?"

She stopped at his feet and smiled. "Every man folds when a woman is involved."

"*Is she alive?*" Jake asked, spitting more blood.

"I don't know. You'll have to ask Birdman."

"Birdman?"

"Birdman." She blew another bubble. "You'll know him soon enough. Funny thing is, you think I'm fucked up, wait until you meet him!"

"Seems you're just someone's monkey, and you're not allowed to kill me, so shall we stop wasting time, and you can take me to the organ-grinder."

The woman laughed. "Quite the tongue on you, eh?" She knelt, lifted one of the legs of her jeans, and exposed a sheath. "I cannot kill you, no, but who's to say I can't have a little fun first?" She slipped out a hunting knife. She stood and circled him again, chewing, moving the knife from hand to hand, and twisting it.

Jake clenched his fists. The hand she'd stamped on before hurt to hell, but he didn't reckon it was smashed as he'd first feared. He'd use it if he got the chance. "Come on, you fucking animal. What you waiting for?"

She darted forward, and he felt pressure on his cheek. He slammed his palm onto his face, as if slapping a mosquito, but she had already withdrawn. His cheek stung. He held his hand in front of his face and looked at the blood on his palm. "Good shot."

"Actually, it wasn't. I was aiming for your eye."

Jake felt his blood boil. "I'm going to kill you."

She came again. This time, she caught his forehead. Again, he slapped it. Again, he missed.

"*Shit!*"

"My thoughts exactly," she said. "Third time lucky?"

Jake bit his tongue and closed his eyes. He tried to tune out everything but the sounds of her movements. He listened to her feet padding on the ground as she circled him.

Wait. Wait.

Her movements were soft and gentle, rhythmic. He was listening carefully for that subtle but sudden change.

Wait. Wait. Wait.

There it was. A slight burst in volume, a slight raise in tempo. He felt the cut on the top of his nose at the same time he slammed his hands together in a clapping motion above his head. He locked onto her wrist. His eyes flicked open. "Gotcha."

He yanked, dragging her on top of him, then flipped over, careful to push her hand and the knife held within to her side.

She was desperately fighting his grip, but he had her pinned to the ground by his weight and strength, which were both superior to hers.

She spat in his face. "It's a shame you won't live long enough to remember me by those scars."

He released her left hand so he could free an arm and drive his elbow into the bridge of her nose. When he saw that she was still conscious, he did it again. Then he slapped her face, checking she was out cold, and rolled off her to catch his breath. His eyes stung as blood ran into them from his broken forehead. Using his sleeve, he tried his best to clear his vision.

The overturned wheelchair.

Piper.

He hoisted himself onto one elbow and wiped at his eyes again—

Bared teeth and red eyes swirled before him. She was coming down on him, knife raised.

His hands found the hilt before she could drive it into his chest. He threw them into another roll, twisting the weapon upward with all his might. When he crashed on top of her again, he forced the blade upward into her neck just beneath her chin. He stared down at her as she gargled blood. He pushed the blade deeper and waited for her eyes to glaze over.

"Fuck!" he shouted, stumbling off her. "Fuck ... fuck ..." He rose to his feet. *What the hell was going on?* He watched the twitching body. These bastards had turned him into some kind of monster.

He swooped again for his tire iron. He spent a minute or two searching for the gun in the thick, tangled undergrowth but came up emptyhanded. Opting not to waste any more time, he drew the knife from the woman's neck and started toward the rocks and the summit.

The journey was arduous. Not only had the last couple of days ripped it out of him, but he was now contending with leaking gashes on his face. His sleeve was drenched with blood, and if he looked anything like he felt, he would be a sight to behold.

First, he worked his way through the mounds of broken rocks. He climbed on top of the first mound, which just about remained stable under his weight, so he could look out over the others for any signs of ambush. From that viewpoint, he couldn't see anyone skulking around the rocks, but he remained incredibly cautious as he wove among the rest.

After the rocks, he ascended the slope to the summit. At a distance, he counted two figures, and when he eventually drew close enough, he identified two men with their backs to him.

And Piper's wheelchair lying there.

He came to within two yards of them. "I'm here." He wiped at his wound again. "Where is she? Where's Piper?"

One man turned. He sported a short mohawk and wore a leather jacket with its sleeves rolled up; his hands and arms were heavily tattooed. He aimed a gun at Jake's chest. "Where is Autumn?"

Jake shrugged. "Who?"

"My wife."

"Jesus." Jake threw a thumb over his shoulder. "That sadist? Your wife?"

The man stepped forward.

"Don't worry. She's alive," Jake lied.

"Mr. Pettman, you're late," the other man said, turning. This man wore a tight vest, highlighting his bulky, muscular build. Unlike the other man, he cared little about his hair, and it sprang up unkempt and tangled on his head. He pointed at the other man. "Austin, you have your instructions. Stand down."

Jake wiped at the blood running into his eyes again and pointed with the hand holding the blade at the two men. "Which one of you killed Peter?"

The muscular man nodded. "That was me."

"You will die today for that," Jake said.

"I see your anger," the man said. "It was what I anticipated. It brought you to me."

"Yes ..." Jake took several steps forward. "And in a moment, you are going to feel it. Where is Piper? If you've harmed her, you'll suffer more than you've ever thought imaginable."

"Now then, Mr. Pettman, I wouldn't go underestimating the extent of my imagination. I would like you to know my name, before the end comes. It is Alpheus Bird."

"Yes, the psychopath back there said you were the Birdman."

"Hold your tongue when talking about my wife." Austin stepped toward Jake with his hand tense on his weapon.

"The sadist?" Jake asked.

Austin took another step.

Alpheus hissed.

Austin stopped.

"Birdman is not my name, Mr. Pettman. It is Alpheus Bird."

"Where. Is. Piper?"

Alpheus turned and pointed off the cliff.

Jake's insides crumpled. "No. I don't believe—"

"I warned you."

Jake's legs felt like they were melting, but he had nothing to lean on, so he stumbled forward instead. "You ... No ... That's not right. Why would you?"

"You are shocked. It is understandable. Shock is a very human response. Part of a rather cluttered nature—"

"This needs to end, Alpheus," Austin said. "Do hawks torture their prey? Let me end this."

"Your emotions are probably high too, Austin. However, interrupt me again, and you, too, will fall."

Jake reached the edge and slid to his knees. None of this felt real. He laid the knife on one side of him and the tire iron on the other, closed his eyes, and pressed his fingers against his temples. *Just let me wake up ... Just let me wake up ... God, I beg of you ...* He opened his eyes and peered over.

And there she lay, maybe twenty yards below, face down. Her dark hair fanned out on the rock she was broken on.

"Not a big fall, but big enough," Alpheus said.

Jake clenched his fists and sensed Alpheus pacing behind him.

"Do you have any idea why I've hunted you, Mr. Pettman?"

Piper, what have I done?

"It seems you have a past. A rather unsavory one, by all accounts. My intention was not to torture you. But you are impressive prey. Arguably, my most impressive to date."

Why Piper? She was innocent. Just like Paul Conway, just like Peter Sheenan.

"It was safer to draw you out, bring you to my territory. And now, seeing you on your knees, I am surprised."

I'm better off dead.

"It's understandable, but still, it remains surprising. I think it's best now to bring this to an end."

But first ... "Can you not see the blood on the knife?" Jake turned and looked at Austin. "It's from your wife. I buried it in her neck."

At first, Austin looked confused, as if he didn't understand what Jake had said.

Jake smiled at him to help the realization along. It worked.

"No!" Austin pounced forward and thrust his boot in Jake's face.

Jake sprawled backward in the dirt.

"Now, that's more interesting," Alpheus said. "More what I expected. Some fight at least. Give me the gun, Austin, and have some time with him before the end."

Jake rolled onto his front into a crouching position. He felt his head burn as Austin took him by the hair and yanked backward. He felt the bastard's lips against his ears.

"I'm going to break your fucking neck." The prick backed off, allowing him time to rise to his feet.

Jake turned so his back was to the cliff edge. "Come on!" He gestured Austin toward him with a wave of his hands.

Austin obliged and came in swinging.

Jake swooped, and the fist drew past his face with a *whoosh*. He slammed his own fist into the assassin's ribs.

Austin gasped for air.

Jake seized his opportunity to deliver several more blows, all to the face. The punches hurt his own knuckles, but, right now, the pain was *satisfying*. Jake had worked them away from the cliff edge with his footwork, removing himself from immediate danger. He chanced a glance at Alpheus.

He watched intently, holding the gun in Jake's direction but had no intention of using it.

"Enjoying?" Jake hissed.

Alpheus simply nodded. It could be an affirmation or just an instruction for Austin to continue. What it did do though was *distract* him.

Austin sent a devastating blow into the side of Jake's head, and the world turned inside out for a moment. He managed to weave away from the following blows, and even feigned that he was about to tumble by intentionally letting his legs buckle, so when Austin came in closer, Jake could deliver a crushing uppercut.

Austin's head snapped backward.

Jake sprang, using the momentum to deliver a splintering left hook. He rode the adrenaline that coursed through him and delivered jab after fierce jab to the bastard's torso. Jake saw Piper's body on the rock; Peter's body in the chair; Paul on the road. His anger burned. He *ached* for release.

Jab-jab-jab.

His knuckles were on fire; it was the most pleasurable pain he'd ever known.

The bastard's head was drooping.

"Lift up your head, fucker."

He didn't.

Jake went in again.

Jab-jab-jab.

Every blow was ecstasy.

Out of breath, Jake staggered backward.

Austin looked unsteady on his feet. He was ready for the taking.

"I'm going to kill you," Jake said and drove forward again.

Austin swooped to the side, caught Jake's wrist, and delivered a blunt elbow to his cheek.

Jake swung out but found only empty air. The elbow came twice more, and an uppercut had Jake on his knees, gasping for air. Austin was raining kicks upon him, and he slumped to his side. The blows were fierce; Jake felt the life being pummeled out of him. He tried to move away, but he realized he was completely spent. So this was it.

I'm sorry, Piper. I'm sorry, Peter.

At least he was about to get what he deserved. He felt Austin's arm loop around his neck. With his oxygen supply severed, Jake couldn't protest. He dug his nails into the tattooed arms, but if his adrenaline levels were anything like his, he wouldn't be feeling it.

"I said I would break your neck. Alpheus?"

Jake felt his world swim.

"Yes," Alpheus said. "Enough is enough. Finish him."

Jake felt the pressure intensify. Darkness closed in.

18

EARLIER

G ABRIEL DRAGGED HIMSELF from the water
and onto the sandy bank with his good hand. He
rolled onto his back, stared up into the blue, and gulped
the air.

It was over.

He glanced at the shoulder that had caught the bullet—
whose, he couldn't say—and stared over the Skweda toward
the boathouse where he'd just swum—or, more accurately,
floundered—from. A place renowned for its quiet and
isolation now beat with life. Helicopters, dogs, officers, and
drowning amongst that chaos was Kayla. And who had
been at the center of it all? The rank outsider, the
wandering devil: Jake Pettman.

Concerned about being spotted from the other side of
the river, Gabriel crawled up the bank and into more
woodland. Wincing and groaning, he wormed to the nearest

tree and propped himself against the trunk. He tugged down his shirt so he could inspect the shoulder wound—a surface wound. It would bleed to hell, just like all his other fucking wounds, but he was reasonably confident it wasn't life threatening. Of course, the infections that would threaten him in the coming days could well be, but that was a bridge for another day.

The bandages wrapped around his damaged hand and the knife wound were sodden. His instinct was to pull them off, but he fought the impulse. It was hot and would surely get hotter as the day wound on. *Leave them to dry.* Freeing his injuries just meant he risked more bleeding.

He closed his eyes. God, was he exhausted. He put his head against the tree and thought of Kayla ...

"Father?" Kayla said.

"Yes, honey?" Gabriel replied.

"I really liked Anna."

Gabriel smiled. He reached across the dinner table and took her hand. He was glad to see his fingers back where they belonged. "Me too. She's funny too, huh?"

"Yep. She's *sharp*. Even after I went to bed, I could hear you two talking until ridiculously late."

Gabriel laughed. "It would have gone on longer, no doubt, if she hadn't had to leave. She needed to be up for work."

"Too right! Surgeons need their sleep."

"I agree." Gabriel waved his fingers in the air. "The miracles they work. Look what Anna did here."

"Unbelievable."

"And look what they did with you, Kayla." He leaned

forward and stroked the cheek Susannah had carved open. "You cannot even tell it happened."

"Technically, that was a laser not a surgeon."

"It's a brave new world." He took her hand again and smiled. "And I'm glad to be sharing it with you."

"And me with you, Father. And Anna too, hopefully; she's so nice. And so *funny*!"

"One step at a time, dear. Why don't you go and get us both a glass of water?" He watched Kayla leave the dining room for the kitchen; he felt his heart gave a little leap. It could have ended so differently. But it hadn't, had it? And now, it couldn't be any more perfect. He called into the kitchen. "I delivered, didn't I, Kayla? I gave you the life I promised you."

"You did, Father!" Kayla shouted in from the kitchen.

He heard the hissing of water from the faucet and the whooshing of two glasses filling. Gabriel wiped tears away. "I don't deserve you, Kayla. I will make sure every moment of your life is blessed."

Five minutes passed, and Kayla did not return.

In every second of those five minutes, Gabriel knew he should go to the kitchen to see if she was all right, but he felt compelled to stay. "Every moment, Kayla."

Ten minutes passed, and still, she didn't return.

"Every *single* moment."

When an immeasurable amount of time had passed, Gabriel rose to his feet. He noticed he lacked energy and was rather unsteady on his feet. He grabbed a walking stick by the kitchen door and caught his reflection in a mirror alongside it. His hair was gone, and his face was wrinkled and pale. He went into the kitchen.

Two glasses of water stood untouched on the sink.

He hobbled to them and stroked the glass, reminiscing

over a period somewhere in the distance recesses of time when someone close to him had touched that glass. He tried to recall her name but could not. He did remember he'd once had a daughter. She'd been beautiful with dark, luscious hair and a fire in her belly the like of which the world had never seen.

He was hungry, so he approached the fridge.

He'd also had a sister too, even further back in that dark corridor of time. He couldn't quite remember what had happened to her, only that he'd loved her with all his being.

He opened the fridge. The body of a young girl was wedged in there. She was grey, and her face was frozen in a sad expression. "Oh, Collette," he said in a voice destroyed by time and pain. "Oh, Collette, I remember now." He reached out and touched the cold body. "And I miss you so."

Gabriel woke to an orchestra of pain. Unwilling to listen, he roared and managed, eventually, to drown it out.

Jake.

He rose to his feet and checked his watch. He'd been asleep for hours.

Jake Pettman.

He reached into his pocket for the medicine bottle, unscrewed it, and tipped the remaining five Adderall into his hand. He sighed with relief when he found the water hadn't ruined them. He dry-swallowed them. This was his heaviest dose to date.

Self-righteous sonofabitch. Since the moment you walked into Blue Falls, my world has crumbled. If you'd left me be, I'd have dealt with Mason Rogers in my way; I'd have found the truth on my terms; I'd never have found myself cornered and forced to run.

With Kayla.

He felt tears in the corners of his eyes.

Beautiful, sweet Kayla. You have stolen her from me.

He took a deep breath and relived those seconds again when he saw Jake charging toward him as he laid Kayla into the boat. He'd stood and looked across the Skweda to the soundtrack of thumping helicopter blades, waiting for the end.

One last shot, he'd thought. *Even with my damaged hands, I can put one between Pettman's eyes.*

But he hadn't, had he? Maybe it was because he'd turned too quick; maybe it was because the rifle rested on his damaged hand; maybe it was *just* the exhaustion of the past days which unsettled his usual steady hands. Whatever the reason, he'd missed.

He surveyed the wound on his shoulder.

Have I been lucky?

He strode through the woodland. With the boathouse to his rear and the sun directly ahead, he knew where he was going now—not far at all.

Lucky?

He snorted. Luck had nothing to do with it. He was alive for a reason. "I'm coming, Jake."

When Gabriel reached the outskirts of Blue Falls, he stopped. There was no way he could just stroll into town. In a residential area, there'd be few people who wouldn't recognize him as a fugitive. And, on the off chance someone *didn't* recognize him, they would probably take one look at the bloody, exhausted state of him and call for the emergency services anyway.

He was close to an old, rundown industrial estate on the edge of town. Only three businesses were currently hanging on in tough economic times and, with any luck on a Sunday, they might just be closed. One of these businesses was a used car dealership.

As hoped for, shutters were drawn in the three businesses, and the estate was quiet. Gabriel came around the edge, trying his best to avoid any surveillance cameras; maintaining the illusion he was dead at the bottom of the Skweda was in his best interests. He also intended to make as little fuss as possible so they'd have little reason to be checking the cameras first thing tomorrow.

When he reached the vehicles in the parking lot of the used car dealership, he chose a beat-up old Volvo on the edge that no one would miss in a hurry. Another reason for choosing the old vehicle was a manual lock. He scoured the ground for a rock, caved in the driver's window, leaned in, unlocked it, and opened the door.

He brushed the glass off the seat into the footwell rather than onto the ground for a car salesman to spot first thing. He wanted the missing Volvo to go unnoticed as long as possible. After sitting in the driver's seat, he put his in-depth knowledge of crime to good use and hotwired the vehicle.

There wasn't a great deal of gas in the car, but he was confident he would have enough to kill Jake and get out of town before needing a refill.

Gabriel needed to do two things urgently: arm himself and eat. He drove slowly down his road and passed his home.

No cars were in the driveway. As he circled round, using the adjacent street, he toyed with the idea of addressing his needs at home sweet home.

Yes, someone might see the Volvo going into the driveway, but would they necessarily think it was Gabriel Jewell, fugitive, or, if the news was out, the ex-chief returned from the dead? The place would have been busy with investigators over the past days, so nosy neighbors might just shrug it off as more of the same?

Fuck it. You know what they say. Hide in plain sight.

He drove to the end of the driveway, turning the vehicle so the driver's door was aligned with the front door as best as he could. He reached into his damp jean's pocket for his door key. He took a deep breath. Leaving the car running, he was out of the driver's door and through the front door before exhaling.

One minute later, he was out of his house and into his vehicle with his spare rifle retrieved from underneath the sofa and a tube of Pringles from the cabinet above the kitchen sink.

The combination of food and Adderall gave Gabriel a clarity he'd been lacking for days. He drove with purpose, filled with the desire and determination to put right so many wrongs. His eyes were continually drawn to the rifle he'd propped against the passenger seat.

After passing the Goodwin's house and seeing their empty driveway, Gabriel followed his instincts to Peter Sheenan's home—Jake's partner in crime.

His heart beat wildly when he saw Jake's rented Ford sitting on the pavement outside the old Indian's house. He drew up several yards behind it. At first, he stopped, one hand flying to the rifle and the other, damaged hand settling on the door handle, but he steadied himself. It was a good thing he had. He observed Jake marching onto the porch. To take him out in such a public a setting wouldn't be conducive to his subsequent escape plan.

He watched the bastard lean over the railing before fiddling with his phone for a time. He looked to be in quite an anxious state. When his target marched down the path back toward his vehicle, Gabriel slipped low into his seat. Hopefully, the prick would be too distracted by his own concerns to notice the running engine on the rusty, old Volvo.

Jake jetted off at quite a good clip.

"What's the rush?" Gabriel asked, putting his foot on the gas pedal.

Again and again, Gabriel bashed his hand against the steering wheel. Eventually, common sense took over. He only had one good hand left, no point in pulverising it. Initially, he'd been doing well, keeping up with the bastard, but then stalled the old Volvo just after a rotary and just before the bridge over the Skweda. After he'd hotwired the Volvo again, he got himself tangled up at some red lights, and the heavy flow of traffic in his path did not offer him a break.

Once he'd broken through, he crossed the Skweda anyway, but then gave up the ghost and pulled over to a quiet spot at the side of the road so he could take out his frustrations on the wheel. He glanced at the rifle and sighed. How long could he realistically linger around with a vendetta? The checkpoint would be down now. His route to freedom unimpeded. A second chance to escape. He could be the winner here.

So, why did it feel like a loss? Another loss in a series of losses?

He looked at himself in the rearview mirror. He stared at his blood-splattered face and tired, aging eyes. "Game over," he said. He finished his Pringles, attempted to calm himself, and opted for the highway—and freedom.

Convinced he was seeing things, Gabriel rubbed his eyes.

Jake's Ford was buckled against the rock at the foot of Ross Hill.

What the hell?

He stopped behind it and, armed with his rifle, exited the Volvo, and circled the vehicle.

Empty.

He turned and looked up the sloped dirt path that led to the summit.

Maybe?

He looked down at the bent fender, then at the highway.

Or he just flagged someone down and was taken to the hospital?

He looked back up the dirt path.

Nothing to lose. Only two minutes out of the way.

As soon as Gabriel entered the parking lot on Ross Hill, it was clear he'd stumbled onto something significant—the two-dead-bodies kind of significant. He brought his car to a crunching halt a suitable distance from the other three vehicles. He left the engine running in case he had to make a quick getaway, popped the door with his good hand, and leaned over to grab his rifle with the same hand. After kicking open the door, he stepped free.

He took a deep breath. The air was cooler up here, invigorating. He welcomed it. It mixed well with the Adderall and the recent sustenance. He slung the rifle over his shoulder and slammed the car door.

He inspected the two bodies. The older man had been shot, while a younger, black man had gotten his skull crushed by a car door. He tried to build a narrative in his head but failed, and so didn't bother trying again. Truth be told, he'd absolutely no idea what was going on.

Jake was involved. That was good enough for him.

He looked across the views of Rosstown Plantation and wondered if it was the last time he'd ever behold this magnificent sight. This was *his* world. He was born here, and, by rights, he should die here. Jake, and all those like him, had taken this privilege away. He narrowed his eyes. He would claim closure now, but he wouldn't underestimate him. He'd seen the man in action, after all.

He looked at the black man's pummeled head again.

Yes. Jake was not a man to be taken lightly.

Through the wooden gate that led to the broken rocks and the summit, on a dirt track among a patch of trees, Gabriel discovered more evidence of the dangerous nature of Jake Pettman—the body of a woman who was mid-twenties at the most. Her chin and chest were wet with blood. The ground around her was sodden, and Gabriel kept his distance to avoid churning the ground into a bloody mud. Her pigtails made her look fragile and innocent.

"What did you *do* to piss off Jake Pettman?"

Gabriel headed toward the broken rocks. He'd been before, of course, many times, so he could negotiate them easily without putting himself in danger of ambush. After the rocks, he glimpsed a small group of people in the distance.

Life.

With three dead and counting, he didn't expect that to last long.

He quickened his pace.

As Gabriel drew closer to the group, a light breeze carried the sound of their commotion over to him.

Grunting.

Closer still, it became clear two of the men were fighting, while another watched several yards away with his back to Gabriel. This allowed him to draw even nearer without being noticed.

Gritting his teeth over the agony of doing so, Gabriel pulled his rifle from his shoulder and supported the muzzle of it with his bandaged left hand. He paused when his eyes finally focused on the taller of the two fighting men.

Jake.

Jake had the initiative in the fight and was landing a series of powerful blows on his opponent.

Gabriel closed the gap, expecting the conflict to end soon, when the exchange took an unexpected turn. Gabriel watched in surprise as the opponent, who'd looked beaten for sure, managed to land a swift couple of elbows, followed by an uppercut. Jake was on his knees, and the man he should have beaten was now pummeling him. As enjoyable as this was to watch, Gabriel didn't want this over before he'd had chance to look him in the eyes, so he increased his pace.

The man slipped around the back of Jake to secure him in a headlock and throttled him.

Adrenaline surged through Gabriel. Jake was not *his* to claim.

He went to his knees. It would allow him a steadier aim. He lifted the rifle, sighted Jake's opponent, and tried desperately to keep still the busted hand supporting the rifle.

Fuck. The agony!

He gritted his teeth, willing for steadiness with every ounce of his being. When it seemed he'd found the briefest moment of stillness between the tremors, he pulled the trigger, certain he'd miss.

The man's head burst.

The pressure on Jake's neck disappeared. Still on his knees, he gasped for air.

Austin fell to the ground beside him, a chunk missing from the top of his head.

Pain raged through Jake. His breathing was out of control. Despite this, he managed to look up at Alpheus, who was staring in the distance. He followed his line of sight to Gabriel, who was quickly approaching.

Alive? How was that possible? Was he hallucinating?

Maybe he was still being strangled? Was this the moment between life and death when the brain goes haywire?

"You, in the muscle vest," Gabriel said. "Throw your fucking gun off the cliff."

Jake watched Alpheus; the gun stayed at his side.

"Last chance before I mix your brain with your friend's over there."

Alpheus still didn't move.

"Suit yourself, you dumb bastard."

Alpheus spun and threw the gun as hard as he could off the cliff.

Jake followed it with his eyes. He thought of Piper lying on the rocks. It made every part of his soul writhe, and it took away his will to stay conscious. He closed his eyes. He was done with this.

"What do you want?" Alpheus asked.

"Him."

Jake opened his eyes.

"Ah. He's a popular man."

"Depends on your definition of the word, *popular*. He hasn't enamoured himself to many around these parts."

"Nor back where he came from either. But you know that already, don't you, Gabriel?"

"How do you know my name?"

"I know it was you who contacted England. That it was you who gave up Jake's location."

Jake felt a surge of anger. "How could you?" Blood dribbled from his mouth. He couldn't be sure if his words were clear.

"Don't blame me for *who* you are!" Gabriel shouted at Jake while keeping his rifle on Alpheus.

Jake spat more blood. "You brought them ... here."

"No! You brought them here. You're the harbinger. Before you came, Blue Falls was—"

"*Broken* ..." Jake managed.

"But peaceful, you sonofabitch, Pettman. *Peaceful.* And my life was as it was."

"*Damaged* ... It was damaged."

Gabriel moved the rifle and sighted Jake. "Say that again."

Jake took a deep inhalation through his nose "And you damage the lives of everyone." Jake saw the butt of Gabriel's rifle coming toward him. Everything flashed. The burning in his cheek was intense. "Everyone." He closed his eyes.

"Gabriel," Alpheus said.

"Be quiet, freak! Do you think you're walking away from this?"

"Gabriel. We *all* want the same thing."

"All?" Gabriel chortled. "You mean me and you; the rest of your merry band are soup!"

"Just me and you, then. At this stage of the hunt, it is better to finish the prey. It no longer bothers me who concludes the kill; we hunted as a pack, *successfully.*"

"What are you talking about?"

"Finish him, Gabriel."

Jake felt the end of the rifle pressing into his forehead.

"On my own initiative, thanks," Gabriel said, "not on yours, freakshow."

Jake reached up and closed his hand around the muzzle. His original intention was to push it away with his flagging strength, but what was the point? The end was here, if Gabriel wanted it so. He was outmanned, on his last legs, and the gunman was riding high on bloodlust and amphetamines. He opened his eyes at the man he'd killed with. "Pull the trigger. Kayla is safe."

"How dare you!" Gabriel bared his teeth.

"She's better off ... without you."

"Shut up, Pettman." He pushed the muzzle of the gun hard into Jake's forehead. "Shut the hell up."

"You know this already." Jake watched Gabriel's face quiver and redden. He felt the muzzle hard against his forehead. He closed his eyes and prepared for oblivion.

When nothing happened, he opened his eyes.

"I wanted to give her a good life," Gabriel said.

"You wouldn't have been able to." Jake paused, coughing. "One day, you will realize that is true."

Gabriel's face dropped.

"Accept," Jake said and spat out more blood. "Accept that it's for the best ... find some peace."

"I can't undo the things I've done."

"No, you can't. I know how that feels."

"This is taking too long," Alpheus said.

"Shut up!" Gabriel turned the rifle from Jake to Alpheus. "You wait as long as necessary."

"What am I waiting for, exactly?"

"Ask me that question again, and I'll give you an answer." Gabriel refocused on Jake but kept the rifle trained on Alpheus. "Tell me about the life she will have."

"I can't answer that."

"Why?" Gabriel creased his brow. "Piper is her sister. She can take care of her."

Jake felt the world turning around him. Why was he still here? Suffering this? Why hadn't he just let Gabriel shoot him when he had the chance? Anything was preferable to the agony inside. "Dead. She's dead."

"What? I don't believe it! How?"

"Ask Alpheus."

Gabriel turned to Alpheus. "What happened?"

"As you're well aware, Gabriel, he is prey that deserves respect. We needed to make special arrangements. Peter, and then Piper, were used to draw him—"

"Just answer the fucking question! What happened to her?"

Alpheus nodded at the cliff.

"No. No way. It doesn't make sense." Keeping the rifle locked on his target, Gabriel shuffled to the edge and looked over.

Jake managed to turn his head; he was regaining some control.

Gabriel eyed Jake, and his expression darkened. He glared at Alpheus and waved the rifle at him. "Get on your knees."

Alpheus smiled. "A red-tailed hawk gets on the ground for no one."

"On. Your. Knees."

Alpheus peeled off his muscle vest and cast it to one side. He turned and showed the large red-tailed hawk on his back.

"You have to be fucking kidding me," Gabriel said.

"Birdman," Jake said and snorted

Alpheus turned back. "My name is—"

"Listen," Gabriel said. "I couldn't give a rat's ass what your name is. But I'll tell you this for nothing." He let the rifle fall to his side, then to the ground. "I'm going to fucking enjoy killing you." He charged.

The two men looped their large arms around each other, went to the ground, and rolled.

Jake wiped blood from his eyes and spied the rifle several yards ahead of him.

Alpheus, lean and dextrous, weaved his way into a

dominant position, straddling Gabriel. The chief of police took two heavy blows to the face.

With his breathing under control, every second was bringing Jake closer to action. He crawled forward to retrieve the rifle.

Gabriel, hulking and strong, flipped the birdman onto his back and drove his fist again and again into his face.

Jake's hands fell onto the rifle.

When Gabriel had reduced Alpheus's face to a mess of blood, he rose. He took two steps backward and put his hands to his knees to catch his breath.

Alpheus sat upright. His face was mangled, but Jake could still see the determination in his eyes.

Gabriel still fought for breath. Delivering a barrage of blows had taken it out of him.

Alpheus put his hands to the floor to support himself, pulled his legs to his chest, and rocked forward into a kneeling position.

Gabriel straightened and waved him up. "Let's finish this, Birdman."

Alpheus moved at an incredible pace. He slipped a blade from an ankle sheath and pounced upward, slamming it into Gabriel's left side just below his ribcage. He slid it out and buried it again. And then again. The skilled assassin's thrusts moved at such a speed it was impossible to count the strikes.

Jake had readied the rifle, but Gabriel's huge frame blocked a clear shot.

When Gabriel stumbled away, clutching his side while blood spilled between his fingers, Jake took his shot.

And missed.

"Shit."

He tried again. The clunk of the rifle indicated an empty chamber.

Alpheus stalked to Gabriel, blood-stained knife poised.

Gabriel was kneeling at the edge of the cliff.

When Alpheus was close enough to cut Gabriel's neck, he said, "On the contrary, I'm going to enjoy killing—" His head jerked backward, his eyes widened, and he exhaled a long, deep groan.

Jake scanned Alpheus for the source of his sudden injury, and his eyes stopped at his groin. Gabriel had reached behind himself and grabbed Alpheus's balls.

Gabriel dragged the bastard forward to the edge.

Alpheus fought by slamming the knife into Gabriel's shoulders, but the chief of police had already instructed his body on what to do, and the adrenaline would see him finish this.

Alpheus's face was contorted with agony.

Gabriel looked up at him. "Fly, little birdie." He thrust Alpheus off the cliff by his balls. "Fly."

There was a short yelp, then several thuds, as Alpheus collided with the rocks jutting from the cliff face.

Gabriel focused on Jake, blood pouring from his mouth. He nodded once, then slumped to his side, his eyes wide but empty.

Exhausted, wounded, and in despair, Jake lay for a time, wondering if he might die. It became clearer with every passing minute that this wouldn't happen, and when his body's desire to live seemed to intensify under the blazing afternoon heat, he got to his feet. His body made some unusual cracking sounds as he straightened up, and he groaned. He wiped blood and tears from his eyes and took a final look over the cliff edge.

Alpheus had fallen significantly farther than Piper, having missed the outcrop of rock which had caught her. He was face up, unlike Piper, and the rock he lay on was dark with blood.

He stared at Piper's body, wondering if things would have turned out differently if he'd never crashed at the bottom of Ross Hill and missed his deadline or, better still, if he'd never even have been fucking born—then his cellphone rang. He read the name on the phone—*Piper*—and looked at the body again.

He creased his brow and answered. "Hello? Who is this?"

"Er ... Piper? Have you deleted my number or something?"

"*Who* is this?" He was struggling to breathe.

"Jake, you're not making any sense."

The world pulsed around him. He lowered himself into a squat to prevent himself from tumbling. He dared to feel some relief ... he forced it back. "It's not possible." He eyed Piper's body. "Where are you?"

"I just left the Holbrooks. I stayed over with Willow last night. She was beside herself over Molly, and Ethan's answer was to drink. They're both asleep now, but I haven't slept a wink."

"So, you haven't been home?"

"I haven't been home since my afternoon shift yesterday. What's wrong, Jake?"

"Your wheelchair?"

"I left it at home. Putting those crutches to good use. Listen, I'm home now."

Jake looked down again, and it dawned on him who it could be.

"That's funny," Piper said.

"*What?*"

"The car on the road outside my house. I'm sure that belongs to—"

19

EARLIER

L ILLIAN HAD THOUGHT about this *all* night.
She'd barely slept a wink. Right now, Jake was
gallivanting around the woods with Peter, playing cowboy.
If Jake continued down this road, he would find himself in
jail; Louise would make damned sure of that. So, if the
stubborn fool wouldn't listen to him, then maybe, just
maybe, he would listen to the woman he loved.

She parked her car on the street opposite the Goodwin
house. She noticed no one was parked in the driveway, and
she wondered if she'd chosen the wrong time to visit. She
gave it a go anyway and approached the front door.

Misty Meadow House.

She took a deep breath and knocked on the door. As she
waited, she ran through what she would say. *You must talk
to him, Piper. Lieutenant Price is serious. If he continues like
this, then …*

No answer.

She tried again and waited a moment longer before determining she had been right when parking. *Wrong time. No one is in.* She turned from the door, and, as she stepped away, she heard it open behind her. *Ah,* she thought, turning back—

Fingers yanked her hair. Agony ripped through her scalp. She reached up to dig her nails into big hands. Too late. They dragged her forward and forced her to her knees.

The door slammed behind her.

She screamed.

A strong hand wrapped around her mouth.

"Scream again, and I'll hurt you. Do you understand?"

Her reply was muffled.

"Just nod," he said.

Under his tight grasp, she struggled to nod, but he must have detected the attempt and released her.

"Your parents have gone out. They are safe. And they can stay that way."

Parents? Who did he think she was? Piper? Lillian opened her mouth to speak, but terror and confusion had locked down her vocal cords.

"Did your parents not give you a key to their house?"

She opened her mouth to speak again but quickly closed it when she realized she might vomit.

"*Speak!*"

"Yes ... *Yes!* I left it here."

"Okay, I see. Piper, I need you to listen carefully to me."

He does think I'm Piper! Her mind whirred. Could she do anything with this information? Should she tell the truth? That she wasn't Piper? That he'd got the wrong person? In fact, every fiber of her being cried out for her to do just that. Was this panic? Yes, and it was stupidity, so she fought back the instinct, because who's to say he wouldn't just kill her there and then if he discovered she wasn't who he thought she was? Then he could simply wait and kill Piper anyway. No, the rational move was to pretend to be Piper, get this monster out of this house, somehow, and keep herself alive.

"If you walk out this door with me without any fuss, then your chances are good."

"Why are you doing this?"

"I think you know the reason."

"I don't understand."

"Do you think a man like Jake Pettman comes without baggage?"

Lillian's blood froze. "What do you mean?"

"You all pretend, don't you? He pretends he can lead a normal life, while you pretend he doesn't have secrets. Life is so much better with clarity, but not now, I don't have time. I need you to come with me."

She'd been planning to comply. Out in the open may have been her best option for escape, but the tone of his voice, the sense he was enjoying this too much, *scared* her. Panic set in again, and without much thought, she went with instinct and bit deep into his hand that still hovered near her mouth.

He didn't yell, but he did snatch away his hand, buying her a moment.

She was up on her legs, sighting the stairs, desperate to continue riding the adrenaline.

She felt his hands in the small of her back, and she missed the bottom step, colliding with the newel post instead. She rolled off it, into a turn, and stood with her back to the stairs, facing her approaching assailant.

He was a large, strong man with an aquiline face. His eyes were dark and sunken.

She heard the crack of her knee before she felt the pain. Her eyes darted down to watch the bastard pull out of his kick. She watched her leg fold the wrong way, and she collapsed to the ground in agony.

"I warned you, Piper. It didn't have to be this way."

She writhed on the floor, staring at her bent leg, misshapen. "*My leg!*" She bashed the back of her head off the bottom step. She was in excruciating pain. Barely able to see through her tears, she blinked several times to sight the bastard on his next move.

He was pushing an empty wheelchair toward her. "A stroke of luck. Your mother's, perhaps?"

"Fuck you," she squeezed out between gritted teeth.

"It will make your ride a lot more comfortable, I think." He knelt beside her. "After I put you to sleep, of course." He wrapped his arm around her neck.

20

AFTER

H E SAID GOODBYE to Lillian in much the same way he'd said goodbye to Peter—on his knees, screaming his apologies. Then, full of guilt and despair, he turned from the cliff edge and called Piper to give her instructions before limping down the slope toward the broken rocks.

He suppressed tears throughout the journey, because it would be so easy to fold, sink to the ground, welcome responsibility for all this bloodshed, and throw himself to the mercy of Louise Price, but he willed himself on, knowing his time in Blue Falls had to end now—in a matter of minutes, in fact. His continued presence here would only attract more beasts. He had to get lost again, *quickly*, before more people he loved died. Only then, when buried deep in shadows again, could he possibly contemplate purgatory over the blood dripping from his hands.

He passed the body of the young woman he'd killed. His detective's mind told him that his DNA would be on her, as it would be on the other two people he had killed, but his options ranged from limited to none.

He'd told Piper to contact the police and report that Gabriel Jewell had stolen his car. He imagined her doing that just now: *"Gabriel Jewell came here. He looked awful. He wanted Jake. Desperate. He was so desperate. I told him he wasn't here. He demanded the keys to Jake's car. He said he needed to get away. I'm sorry. I gave them to him. It seemed safer that way. It seemed like the only way."*

The problem was that no traces of Gabriel Jewell would exist in his smashed-up Ford, but he had an idea for that—a paper-thin idea. But he was limited, so limited, on options.

He reached the parking lot and sighed in relief when he saw what he'd been hoping for. *Another vehicle. The exhaust pumping.* Gabriel Jewell's stolen Volvo was Jake's way out.

Jake looked sadly at the old man who'd come to his aid, then popped his trunk. Yes, he'd be leaving fingerprints. Yes, they would put two and two together one day; how could they not? But, for now, he just had to concentrate on getting away with as little heat as possible. An identity change would be called for, no doubt, but at least he had the money for that.

He grabbed the jerrycan and was again relieved when he heard the gas sloshing around inside. He jumped into the Volvo—*Jesus, Gabriel, could you not have opted for something better?*—and rattled off downhill. At the bottom of the hill, he sloshed gas all over the inside of his hired ford.

"Burnt out when you crashed it, Gabriel," he said. He pulled out the Zippo. "Thanks, Peter." He set fire to the passenger seat and darted backward when it ignited with an almighty *whoosh*.

As he drove away in Gabriel's stolen car, he watched his rental car burn in the rearview mirror, hoping and praying he'd bought himself enough time to shrug off Blue Falls forever.

———

Piper met him at her front door with two duffel bags. "My God, Jake," Piper said, holding him by his upper arms. "I'm calling an ambulance."

Jake shook his head. "If you call an ambulance, you'll be visiting me in jail for the rest of my life."

"At least I'll get to see you."

He kissed her. His lips stung. Every part of him stung. "When I get somewhere new, I'll contact you."

"You're lying."

Yes, he was. He kissed her again. "Piper, I've made mistakes, so many mistakes."

"You're a good man. You brought my sister back."

"I brought the devil to Blue Falls, and Peter and Lillian are gone, and I-I thought I'd lost you too."

She stroked his battered cheek.

He winced.

"You didn't."

"I have to go. There's a fire on the main highway. I can weave around it now, but if I leave it too long, when they realize Gabriel couldn't have done all this alone, those roads will be full—same as they were when Kayla was missing." He wiped away Piper's tears. He opened the bag to remove some money.

Piper touched the back of his hand. "No, I—"

"Get you and Kayla a place." He handed her several rolls of fifty-dollar bills. "It's what you both deserve." Jake stumbled to his car and slung both duffel bags into the back seat. He turned back. "I almost forgot. Peter's dog. He'll need a home."

"He'll have a home with us."

"Thank you." He took a deep breath. "And Piper?"

"Yes?"

"I'm *so* sorry."

"I love you, Jake."

"I love you too." He jumped in the driver's seat and drove away. When he looked in the rear-view mirror, he watched her steady herself against the doorframe, knowing he would never see her again.

THREE DAYS LATER

LOUISE'S HEAD THROBBED. She popped two Tylenol and sat behind her desk with her head in her hands. Outside, on the department floor, she heard the hustle and bustle of the Blue Falls' officers as they attempted to get to the bottom of what had transpired on Ross Hill. Noise didn't necessarily indicate hard work though, and, in this instance, it most certainly indicated chaos.

The pain of losing both Ewan and Lillian within the space of a week had thrown her own mind into disarray. A permanent well of sadness resided inside her over the loss of her own family but losing those two colleagues had just made it all the deeper. She considered her irrational response to the victims in Susannah Gott's hut and feared, intensely, that more such breakdowns were on the cards. Maybe she should take some time off ...

Her phone rang. "Yes," she answered, still rubbing her temples with her eyes closed.

It was the desk sergeant. "Ma'am, I have a Lieutenant Moore from Maine on the line."

She opened her eyes and stood. "Patch him through. ... Alan?"

"Louise. Have I got you at a good time?"

No. "Yes, of course, Alan. What's the problem?"

"This'll be a bolt from the blue, I know you got your hands full, some kind of serial killer and a shoot out in town I hear?"

"Alan?"

Alan sighed. "I'm sorry, Louise, to call you in these circumstances, but I really wanted you to hear this from me."

Her heart beat wildly. She could hardly breathe. "You found them?"

He didn't reply.

"Talk to me, dammit!"

"They found Robert."

"Dead?"

"Yes, I'm afraid so."

She clawed at her hair with one hand and ran her fingers over her tearful eyes. "My children? Alan, my children?"

"No. Only Robert."

"How did ... How did he die?"

"I don't have all the details. I'm not sure cause of death

has been established. I just wanted you to hear about it from me first."

"Where?"

"Bronwyn."

"Bronwyn?"

"A small town. A couple hours north from where—"

"I know where it is! Why there?"

"I don't know, Louise, but we will find out."

"Do they need me to ..." The words stuck in her throat. She coughed them out. "Identify the body?"

"The remains are decomposed. They've used dental records. I suggest you sit tight, and I will update you when—"

She put down the phone and reached for her car keys.

———

Kayla sat on the edge of the bed in the spare room and stared at a pastel painting of the River Skweda above her bed. She reached to touch the bandage on her face.

"Try not to touch it, dear," Piper said from the doorway.

"Sorry," Kayla said and let her hand fall to her lap.

"Don't apologize. It must be irritating as hell. But if we let it heal without complication, they said they'll stand a better chance of making it less noticeable." Piper entered and sat in a chair beside the bed. She was holding a plastic bag. "I managed to get some of the things you asked me for."

Kayla's eyes widened. "Morris?"

"Morris? Who's Morris?"

Kayla reached for the bag. She thrust her hand inside and retrieved a toy monkey. "Morris with one eye of course!" Technically, Morris had two eyes, but one hung to his chest by a thread and so had obviously been written off as defunct.

"We could fix that eye."

"But then he wouldn't be Morris with one eye!"

"A-ha." Piper smiled. "Fair point." Piper sat back and watched Kayla become reacquainted with her favorite toy.

Even though Kayla was fourteen and had seen and experienced things that most wouldn't—or, at least, *shouldn't*—experience in a whole lifetime, she suddenly seemed like a little girl. And why not?

Maybe innocence doesn't die, Piper thought. *Maybe it just hides until the bad stuff goes away.*

"My real mother gave it to me. She died."

"I know. I'm sorry."

"I thought I didn't have anyone left."

"And that must have been horrible, but you do, Kayla." Piper leaned forward and put a hand to the good side of Kayla's face. "And not just me either. You know I have a good mother and father here too. They took care of me when I could no longer be in that same world you were in. We will take care of you. All three of us. In fact, we will *all* take care of each other. Having a sister is about the best thing that has ever happened to me."

Kayla smiled, and a tear streaked her face. "He said he loved me."

"I know, honey, but now is not the time."

"And he did."

"That might be so, but he was a very confused man."

Kayla nodded. "Will you take me to his grave one time?"

"Why?"

"I want to forgive him. I want to forgive him for what he did to my brother and what he did to me."

"If that's what you would like."

Kayla nodded, and another tear ran down her face.

Piper embraced her, taking care to avoid her wound. *Thank you, Jake. Thank you for bringing her home.*

FIVE DAYS LATER

On the fifth night, in his fifth motel, Jake looked in the bathroom mirror and decided he was appearing marginally human again. As he climbed into bed, he also noticed that, despite the moaning and groaning, he was also moving like his old self.

He stared at the ceiling, wondering, as he'd done every night since leaving Blue Falls, whether it was now time to formulate a plan. So far, he'd just headed north. He'd ditched the old Volvo on the first day and bought another jalopy for cash, but apart from that moment of rational thought, the rest of the time had been spent pretty much on autopilot.

He sighed and decided against a plan. He was just feeling too damned guilty about Peter and Lillian for one. In fact, he didn't dare have one, in case he succeeded. He didn't *deserve* to succeed.

Later that night, he woke in a cold sweat. Ignoring the stiffness and pain, he threw himself from the bed and scurried to one of the duffel bags that Piper had packed for him. *How could I have forgotten?* He removed all the clothes from one bag. He undid all the zips and shook it out.

Nothing.

No! It was all he had left.

He opened the other bag full of money, tipped it onto the floor, and again tore open the zips. And there they were, poking out. "Thank you, Piper, thank you so much for remembering."

He pulled out the photographs. They slipped from his grasp and scattered on the floor. He didn't care; he'd never felt such relief. He grabbed at a photograph of Frank in a Southampton FC shirt—his boy. Another photograph lay in the pile, one he didn't recognize. He looked at the selfie of him and Piper together, raising a glass. He pinned it, along with the picture of Frank, to his chest and flopped onto the floor.

And cried.

SALISBURY, ENGLAND

"What are we doing here?" Emma Gardner asked.

"Good question," DCI Michael Yorke said from the driver's seat. "Don't know. Just had a feeling something was wrong."

Yorke pulled alongside Sheila Pettman's home. As had been the case for a few months now, two cars were in the driveway. Sheila had moved on from Jake—or, more specifically, had moved someone *in*.

"Something wrong!" Gardner said and chortled. "I get you fancy yourself as a rather cool cat, Mike, but that really is the understatement of the year. Something's been very wrong for over a year now, ever since your best friend disappeared into the ether."

Yorke nodded; she was right.

"Have you ever heard from him? Bet you have!"

"No," Yorke lied.

"Would you tell me if you had?"

Yorke looked at her, a ghost of a smile on his lips.

A short man in a suit and tie strolled past. His hair was neatly clipped, and his skin was darkly tanned. He stopped by a lamppost and leaned against it, as if out of breath. He stared up at Sheila's home.

"What's he doing?" Gardner asked.

"Don't know. I'll find out." Yorke climbed out of the car and crossed the road. "Excuse me?" Yorke said, holding up his identification.

The smaller man turned. "Yes, Officer?"

"What are you doing?"

"Catching my breath. It's been quite a morning. My dog ran earlier, and I've been looking ever since. If it carries on like this, I'll have to get the pictures up all over these"—he patted the lamppost behind him—"this afternoon."

"I'm sorry. I hope it works out." Yorke crossed the road and got into the car. "Just lost his dog."

"He probably thinks you've lost your mind."

Yorke drove away, smiling. "Any longer in the car with you, Emma, and I might just do that."

———

Walter Divall, lawyer for the criminal organisation Article SE, watched the police officers drive away. *Yes, I've lost a dog, alright.*

He took out his phone and scrolled through the police photographs of the four dead assassins that one of his many contacts in American law enforcement had emailed to him. *A very vicious dog indeed.*

He looked up at Sheila Pettman's home. *One that needs to be put down.*

FREE AND EXCLUSIVE READ

Delve deeper into the world of Wes Markin with the
FREE and **EXCLUSIVE** read, *A Lesson in Crime*

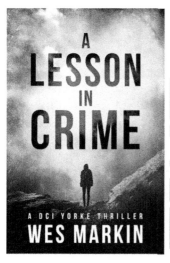

Scan the QR to
READ NOW!

A damaged ex-detective. A pastor hellbent on change. A hidden community born from violence.

And a mysterious young woman whose life hangs in the balance.

Determined to hide himself from a world that has given him only pain, ex-detective Sergeant Jake Pettman plans to stay on the move. That is, until he happens upon Mossbark County and the mysterious young woman, Celestia.

Following a brutal murder, he fails to silence his old police instincts, and his desire for answers lead him into the Nucleus. A sinister, hidden community with a savage history.

And what Jake finds there, will shake him to the very core.

The Rotten Core is an adrenaline-pumping crime thriller from the Amazon bestselling author of One Last Prayer for the Rays, The Killing Pit and the DCI Yorke series. Perfect for fans of Chris Carter, James Patterson, Chris Brookmyre, and Stuart Macbride.

Scan the QR to
READ NOW!

"An explosive and visceral debut with the most terrifying of killers. Wes Markin is a new name to watch out for in crime fiction, and I can't wait to see more of Detective Yorke." – *Bestselling Crime Author Stephen Booth*

The disappearance of a young boy. An investigation paved with depravity and death. Can DCI Michael Yorke survive with his body and soul intact?

With Yorke's small town in the grip of a destructive snowstorm, the relentless detective uncovers a missing boy's connection to a deranged family whose history is steeped in violence. But when all seems lost, Yorke refuses to give in, and journeys deep into the heart of this sinister family for the truth.

And what he discovers there will tear his world apart.

The Rays are here. It's time to start praying.

The shocking and exhilarating new crime thriller will have you turning the pages late into the night.

"A pool of blood, an abduction, swirling blizzards, a haunting mystery, yes, Wes Markin's One Last Prayer for the Rays has all the makings of an absorbing thriller. I recommend that you give it a go." — *Alan Gibbons, Bestselling Author*

One Last Prayer is a shocking and compulsive crime thriller.

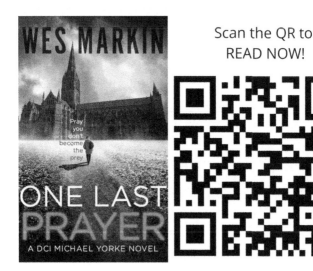

Scan the QR to
READ NOW!

Still grieving from the tragic death of her colleague, DCI Emma Gardner continues to blame herself and is struggling to focus. So, when she is seconded to the wilds of Yorkshire, Emma hopes she'll be able to get her mind back on the job, doing what she does best - putting killers behind bars.

But when she is immediately thrown into another violent murder, Emma has no time to rest. Desperate to get answers and find the killer, Emma needs all the help she can. But her new partner, DI Paul Riddick, has demons and issues of his own.

And when this new murder reveals links to an old case Riddick was involved with, Emma fears that history might be about to repeat itself...

Don't miss the brand-new gripping crime series by bestselling British crime author Wes Markin!

What people are saying about Wes Markin...

'Cracking start to an exciting new series. Twist and turns, thrills and kills. I loved it.'

Bestselling author **Ross Greenwood**

'Markin stuns with his latest offering... Mind-bendingly dark and deep, you know it's not for the faint hearted from page one. Intricate plotting, devious twists and excellent characterisation take this tale to a whole new level. Any serious crime fan will love it!'

Bestselling author **Owen Mullen**

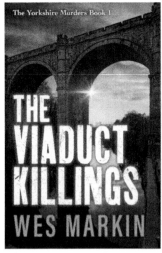

Scan the QR to
READ NOW!

ACKNOWLEDGMENTS

I originally planned Jake's story to be a trilogy, and *Blue Falls* was to be the conclusion. However, after confronting the pathos of Jake's final scene in the motel room, the idea for *The Rotten Core* hit me like a ton of bricks, and I realised that this tale was far from done.

While I was writing *Blue Falls*, I soon realised that Jake was heading onto an action-packed adventure, and that the slower, steadier build-up present in some of my earlier books was absent. To ensure this newer approach worked, I fell back on my support group who, as always, helped me get my vision onto the page.

Firstly, I would like to thank my wife, Jo; my children, Hugo and Beatrice; my entire supportive family; and my close friends.

Thank you to my team of readers who looked at early drafts which included Jo Fletcher, Jenny Cook, Katherine Middleton, Karen Ashman, Dee Groocock, Keith Fitzgerald, Claire Cornforth, Carly Markin, Paul Lautman, and Holly Sutton. Thank you to my fantastic US editor, Brian Peone. All of my ARC readers, and those fantastic bloggers who always get behind me – Shell, Susan, Caroline, Jason and Donna. Thank you to Cherie Foxley for the atmospheric cover.

A special thank you to Donna Wilbor who set up an exclusive group to organise my growing number of advanced readers.

I hope you all join me in February when a tired, and desperate Jake Pettman seeks refuge in Moss County, only to discover the Nucleus – the rotten core of an old land.

STAY IN TOUCH

To keep up to date with new publications, tours, and promotions, or if you would like the opportunity to view pre-release novels, please contact me:

Website: www.wesmarkinauthor.com

facebook.com/WesMarkinAuthor

instagram.com/wesmarkinauthor

twitter.com/markinwes

amazon.com/Wes-Markin/e/B07MJP4FXP

REVIEW

If you enjoyed reading **_Blue Falls_**, please take a few moments to leave a review on Amazon, Goodreads or BookBub .

Printed in Great Britain
by Amazon